A Pilgrimage
to
Guadalupe

A Pilgrimage to Guadalupe

THE FINAL JOURNEY OF THE SOUL

A New Platonic Dialogue

Swami Kriyananda

Crystal Clarity Publishers
Nevada City, California

Crystal Clarity Publishers, Nevada City, CA
Copyright © 2013 by Hansa Trust
All rights reserved.

Printed in China

ISBN 978-1-56589-269-9
ePub ISBN 978-1-56589-514-0

Library of Congress Cataloging-in-Publication Data

Kriyananda, Swami
A pilgrimage to Guadalupe : the soul's final journey / by Swami Kriyananda.
FIRST EDITION
p. cm.
Includes bibliographical references and index.
ISBN 978-1-56589-269-9 (pbk. : alk. paper) -- ISBN 978-1-56589-514-0
(epub : alk. paper)
1. Pilgrims and pilgrimages--Fiction. 2. Guadalupe, Our Lady of--Fiction.
3. Conduct of life--Fiction. 4. Imaginary conversations--Fiction. 5. Religious
fiction. I. Title. II. Title: Soul's final journey.

PS3611.R59P55 2011
813'.6--dc22

2012002116

www.crystalclarity.com
800-424-1055
clarity@crystalclarity.com

COVER AND INTERIOR DESIGN BY MOLLY HERON

Contents

Foreword

AVE YOU EVER HAD WHAT SEEMED TO BE A chance encounter with someone who uplifted and changed you?

In *A Pilgrimage to Guadalupe* the pilgrim experiences a series of just such seemingly chance meetings. As the pilgrim seeks answers to life's deepest questions, those he encounters include—at different times—an atheist, believers, a social activist, Catholic monks, a materialist, and two saintly women.

The author, Swami Kriyananda, a man of remarkable insight and love for humanity, creates compassionate dialogue between the pilgrim and those he meets (whose views of life often differ radically from his own). These conversations are respectful, good-humored, and at times challenging and thought-provoking. Because of the pilgrim's deep respect for each person, each encounter is one of true and open communication; in the process, lives are changed.

People often have beliefs that limit their joyful experience of life. I've read that 71% of Americans believe God is angry, judgmental, or distant. Only 23% of Americans believe in a benevolent God. The pilgrim's first encounter is with "believers" who tell him Jesus Christ came to save us from God's vengeance. The pilgrim replies to his friends, "I don't think Jesus wanted to protect us from God's wrath. He wanted to open us to God's love." He goes on to remind them that Jesus scolded only the hypocrites; he showed compassion for those who sincerely wanted to change. How could God—the father of Jesus—be so radically different from His son?

As you, the reader, accompany the pilgrim on his journey, you will find your own mind expanding. In *A Pilgrimage to Guadalupe* you'll discover a universal, loving, and liberating life philosophy that thrills the soul.

Because Swami Kriyananda's own life, since childhood, has been a pilgrimage, he is well qualified to guide others on the path of truth and awakening. Take up your staff, if you will, and travel with Kriyananda to new vistas of truth, inner joy, and freedom.

You'll be very happy you did.

—JOSEPH CORNELL (NAYASWAMI BHARAT)
Author of *Sharing Nature with Children*
and *AUM: The Melody of Love*

A Pilgrimage
to
Guadalupe

ONE

At the Graveside

THE MOURNERS HAD LEFT. THE COFFIN HAD BEEN lowered to its final resting place; it was now decently covered with dirt. I stood there alone in the darkening twilight, weeping.

"Why?!"

My anguished cry rang out into the gathering night, and in my own heart.

"My beloved wife! Only two days ago I saw your face: smiling, radiant, fresh! I held your hand; it was warm. Now it is cold—dark; beyond my despairing reach!

"Why?"

Intensely I felt her loss. But I wasn't asking, "Why did I lose her?" I knew the answer to that question: The end of life is death. My anguish arose from the thought, rather, "Why do we have to live at all?"

We are born, I reflected, without our conscious consent.

We are driven helplessly onto a stage and forced to play our parts. Whether we play them well or badly seems equally pointless: their ending, in any case, is death. Why even play the game? We can never win it.

Role after role! Game after game! Fresh, exuberant life— then the final sinking into death! Is anything real?

And yet—I thought again—life persists! Is life, and not the countless forms it assumes, the reality?

I thought of life rising up out of the ground, as if with eternal impulse. And then the further thought came: Surely that life contains intelligence, even if it is a different kind of knowing from our own. Is such an awareness possible?

Perhaps we come on earth as exiles from another reality. A higher one?

Ah! Suddenly I felt myself here on earth a stranger—a foreigner, and alone. What could I do? Where could I go? I raised my gaze questioningly above that lonely grave, and looked beyond it.

There, all of a sudden: Lo! I beheld before me a beautiful young girl.

"Why are you here at this lonely site?" I asked her. "Did you know my wife? Have you, too, come to mourn her death?"

She answered me with a smile, "I knew her. I still know her. And I know you!"

"But how is that possible? I have never seen you before! Surely you couldn't know me!"

"My child," she said—and she seemed hardly half my age!—"you have known Me in countless forms. You knew not that it was I, smiling at you behind every happy experience, and weeping with you behind every pain. It was I in the comfort of your mother's arms, holding you when your friends turned away from you. It was I in them also, telling you silently through their disdain: 'Not here will you find the balm you seek.' It was I now, also, who took from you your beloved wife in order that you might know a higher love."

"Then . . . ?" I queried, not daring to pursue the question further in words.

"Yes, I am that life for which you are longing. I am that 'intelligence,' which is much more than arid reasoning: I am absolute Knowledge. And I am absolute Peace, Love, and Bliss!"

My heart burst then, like a broken dam. Waters of pure love gushed out from it in a mighty torrent. "Then You must be that Being whom all men worship! You must be . . ."

"I am your Lady of Guadalupe," She finished for me. It was an unexpected reply. Where was Guadalupe? Who was the Lady there? Why would She come to me?

"I am the Divine in its aspect of Mother," She explained further. "In this form I particularly watch over God's children in the Americas. I am *your* Divine Mother. And you are My divine child."

"Oh, can I be with You always? Always!"

"My son, that is your destiny. But you must first undergo purification. If you would be with Me, you will have to travel. Go as a pilgrim to My shrine in Mexico. Go, as a penitent, by foot."

"Gladly!" I cried. "Shall I then leave everything behind me?"

"Everything, My child. Has anything ever been yours, anyway? Your work, possessions, friends—all these, in the sense that they were yours at all, were yours only on loan. Lo! all things are but gossamer—blowing lightly on the wind."

"Oh, I will leave today! I will leave at this very moment. The thought that You will be waiting there to receive me!"

"Go, then, by narrow roads, avoiding the congested highways. Solicit no rides, but if people offer you a ride, you may accept. Through them you will learn what you need to know."

She smiled kindly, then vanished. I turned away from the grave.

And there before me lay the first stretch of my long journey.

TWO

I Set Forth on My Pilgrimage

I SET OUT WITH ONLY THE CLOTHES ON MY BACK. THE little money I had already on my person was all I took with me. I telephoned no one. My mood was simply to drop out of view, to *be* no one—to cease, in a sense, to exist. I suppose, for me, it was a kind of suicide. Tragic loss had made me want to erase my very identity. "Someday," I thought, "I, too, must die, and those whom I knew best on earth will know me no longer. If someday, then why not now? My true home has never been here. Always, it has been eternity."

Yet despite this thought I set out with hope in my heart. The past was now dead. The future beckoned me with hope of an unknown, but shining, fulfillment. I had leapt off a precipice, having been promised I'd be caught in the air, so to speak. What would happen now?

As I walked down the road, I sang under my breath, the song resounding in my own heart: "Night and day, night and day, dancing, Mother, in Thy joy!"

A car stopped beside me.

"Would you like a ride, friend?" A man in his middle fifties smiled at me as he called out from an open window. I opened the front door of his car and got in.

"Where are you headed?" he asked as soon as I'd got settled. He glanced at me briefly before returning his attention to the road.

"I'm on a search," I replied.

"A search, eh? What are you seeking for?"

"I'm seeking understanding," I said. (What else could I say? It was the simple truth.)

"'In all thy getting,'" he quoted, "'get understanding.' That's in the Bible, you know. Proverbs 4:7. Do you read the Bible?"

"Sometimes," I replied. "I'm sort of familiar with it."

"Friend, all the answers are written there. Say, what's your name? Mine's John, by the way."

"For the moment, I have no name. You might call me Friend."

"Friend, eh? Well that's easy enough. But amnesia! That's a pity. Maybe I can help you. Where are you coming from?"

"What I mean is, I'm trying to forget my past."

"Voluntary amnesia, eh? I've never heard of that syndrome before."

"And yet, if you want to restructure your life completely, the past can be a burden for you."

"Oh, yeah, I get you: sin. That weighs heavy on us all. But even if we forget our own sins, God remembers them! And He doesn't forgive them, either, except through Jesus Christ. Forget? Ha! Not God! Everything we've ever done is held against us at the latter day. Brother, you may fool yourself, but you can't fool God!"

"I should have explained, it isn't guilt that makes me want to forget the past. It's that I want to develop a new life—to start it completely anew—to get a fresh slant on everything. Tell me, however, do you think God really cares very much about the little mistakes we make, so long as we do our best?"

"Listen, even our best is not good enough for Him! God *hates* sin. It's right there in the Bible. 'Mistakes'—ha! *We* may call them mistakes, but our well-meant blunders will take us sliding down to hell every time!"

"Well, but then tell me this: Does God's hatred for sin mean that He hates *us*, if we commit it?"

"Why not? You've heard it said that one is what one eats. If that's true, it must also be true that one *is* what one does."

"So then, if a drunkard bumps into people when he walks, does that mean his act of aggression is held against him? And if a blind man, turning around, knocks a little child to the ground by accident, does that make him a child beater?"

"Ha! ha! I get your meaning. Say, you're a sharp one! I tell you what. Why don't you stop by our house for dinner? The wife will be happy to know you, too."

"I'm happy to accept your invitation," I replied.

"Listen, you say you want understanding. Well, the Bible has it all. Any question you might have, the answer's right there, in the Bible. Oh, I don't mean questions like, 'How many galaxies are there?'—factual stuff like that—but the important questions, like what is life, and how should we live it: It's all there."

"Very well, then, here's a challenge: What *is* life?"

At this question, he fumbled verbally. "Life—well, life is what we're living right now! It's—I don't know; it's being. It's being able to think, and move, and get things done."

I turned the tables on him. Before he could quote the Bible at me again, I pulled it on him myself: "Jesus," I said, "told people, 'I came that ye might have life, and have it more abundantly.' What do you suppose he meant?"

John seemed taken aback. "Meant? Well, gosh, I suppose he meant he wanted us to enjoy life more."

"That? or might he perhaps have meant that he wanted us to enjoy the *sensation* of life, while we live it? the *feeling* of energy, for example, behind our movements? the thrill behind getting things done?"

"Why, that's intriguing! I must say, I haven't really given much thought to what he meant in that passage. But the whole thing's quite simple. It's all spelled out there, as I said. Jesus said, 'Believe on me.' And I believe. He's taken all my sins onto his shoulders. Brother, I don't need to worry about a thing. When I die, I'll go to heaven, be handed my harp, and there I'll be, singing away through eternity with the angels." He threw his head back as if imagining himself shouting hymns of praise in a great chorus. He didn't sing, however.

"Can you really want to do that? From what I hear of your speaking voice," here I smiled to let him know I was not criticizing, "I wonder whether you'd make much of a singer!"

My companion laughed. "Me? Oh, I was only speaking figuratively! No, I'm no singer. I'm tone deaf. What I really mean is, eternity in heaven will someday be mine. And I'm saying also, the road to heaven is *belief.*"

"Belief in what?"

"Why, in the Bible, of course! Belief in the Word of God."

"The Word of God," I said reflectively. "Are you sure that man hasn't sometimes also added to it a few words of his own?"

"How could he? Every word in that Book of books is sacrosanct."

"But it's written on physical paper, and paper can be scribbled on. Here's what I'm asking: Is every word in the Bible just what was originally written there? Don't forget, what we have today is only a translated version, anyway. Look, I'm not trying to argue. But I don't want to be irrational. Jesus is quoted in the Bible as saying, 'He who will not take up his cross and follow me is not worthy of me.' Yet he himself, at that time, had not yet been crucified, and the question of crucifixion hadn't even arisen. The disciples wouldn't have known what he was talking about. Obviously, some scribe had to have inserted that word, 'cross,' later on. Maybe it sounded stronger to him than the teaching that had actually come down to him."

"Hmm," said John reflectively. "I'm not deaf to reason, though I admit theology's not my strong suit. I'll have to talk to my pastor about that. But the main thing is, Christ died for my sins. That's enough for me. I'm cleansed. I've accepted him. I'm one of the chosen few. Yessir!" he continued ardently. "I joined our church when I was twenty-five, and since that time I've never looked back. What church do you belong to, Friend?"

"I'm a member of no church," I replied. "As I said earlier, I'm seeking understanding. To join a church, it seems to me, means to accept its explanations. But I want to understand things for myself. And what am I to understand when I'm told, for example, that Christ died for my sins? Suppose I killed somebody. That's a sin. I need to learn important lessons from it. For one thing, I need to learn that that person, too, was a child of God. In killing him, therefore, I killed God's child. How, then, could I speak of sincerely loving God? It wouldn't be enough that Jesus absolved me of the punishment that awaited me. In that absolution, I'd be deprived of the chance to learn a very important lesson. I'd have also to absolve myself!"

"But the punishment wouldn't be a lesson. It would be God's act of revenge for sinning against His laws."

"Revenge! And what benefit would God himself accrue by vengeance? And as for His laws: How do we learn what those laws are?"

"Why, by reading the Bible!"

"And if I can't read? Is God only for the erudite? Or what about rules that apply today, owing for instance to modern traffic conditions, that couldn't possibly be in the Bible? For instance, a left turn into heavy traffic without giving a proper signal: that might even be a criminal offense today, but what does the Bible have to say about it?"

"Oh, my God! Of course we have to use our common sense also."

"Yes, but my common sense may give me answers on situations that weren't so different from those in Biblical times, situations that aren't discussed in the Bible. Here's a question: Jesus gave us the Beatitudes, but he gave us no comparable maledictions. He didn't say, for instance, 'Cursed are the slanderers, for they shall be vilified.' He might have done so, but the whole emphasis of his mission was on love. Yet his followers today too often emphasize his vengeance!"

"Not at all!" John cried. "We emphasize how his love for us *protects* us from God's vengeance. Why don't we go back to basics? Christ died on the cross for our sins, and all who believe on him shall be saved. That's all there is. What more do you need?"

"And I'm saying that if he, as God's representative, presented God as a Being of anger and vengeance, he had also to partake of these qualities. Yet we see that he was soft on publicans and sinners. It was the law-bound Pharisees he spoke against. When the woman was taken in adultery, he didn't just say to her, 'You are evil!' He said, 'Go, and sin no more.' And to her accusers, he didn't support them in their accusations. Instead, he said, 'Let him who is without sin cast the first stone.' Then he stooped and wrote in the sand. I think what he wrote there was each individual person's special sin who came over to him and looked to see what he was doing: 'Thief! Liar! Bearer of false witness! Cheat!' I don't think Jesus wanted to protect us from God's wrath. He wanted to open us to God's love. His teachings emphasize our need to purify ourselves. He *still* wants to redeem us. But he wants to do so if *we ourselves* want redemption. God's grace does it for us in the end, but we have to open ourselves to that grace. We have to learn *why* it is wrong to kill. We have to learn—by hard experience, often—*why* one should love one's neighbor as one's self."

"Well," John said, "I'm a reasonable man, and what you're saying makes sense."

"The sunlight on the side of a building," I continued, "can enter only into rooms whose curtains are drawn open to receive it."

"And that's what *I'm* saying: Belief it is which draws open those curtains."

"But belief isn't an act. I can stand in the middle of the room and *believe* the curtains to be open. Does that make them so?"

"Well, no, but by belief we *let* Jesus Christ open them for us!"

"And why should he do that? Aren't we capable of doing at least that much ourselves?"

"And why should *I*? He knows it's part of the bargain!"

"Bargain. Is this some kind of marketplace?"

"No, I mean it's part of the deal—the agreement; the promise."

"Why bring it down to that level? Aren't we talking here of divine love? Can any conditions be placed on that love?"

"Okay," he came back at me. "So you say it's his love that absolves me. Sure. The thing is, I'm free from sin now."

"Free in what way? Have you the understanding, now, that enables you to love everybody? Would you help your competitor in business, if he were failing? Might you not rather be pleased at his failure? And would you be tolerant of one whose beliefs contradicted your own?"

"Well, no, there are things, certainly, that I can't tolerate."

"And even if you learned to tolerate other people's opinions, would you be able to tolerate other people's *in*tolerance?"

Reflectively then, he answered, "I see what you mean. It isn't enough to be released from the consequences of our mistakes. We need also to have learned from those mistakes, so that we won't commit them again. I wonder if God's punishment doesn't mean simply *correction*, rather. A mother whose little child tries to dart out into traffic won't just call to him, 'Come back, Johnny! You might get hurt.' She yanks him back, and maybe gives him a paddling to teach him never to do it again. My goodness, you're making me look at things in a whole new way. Maybe Jesus didn't mean what we think. Maybe he only meant, 'I'll help to shoulder your load, and give you strength so you can walk the long journey and make it all the way to the end.'"

"There, I think, you have it! Without God's grace, without His sustenance and inner guidance, the path to perfection would be too arduous. But Jesus himself said the goal of life is perfection. His own words were, 'Be ye therefore perfect, even as my Father is perfect.' And—is even heaven itself perfection?"

"Wow! Listen, I'm driving this car. Let's wait till we get to my home. I'm likely to drive off the road thinking about all these things!"

We drove in silence for awhile. For my part, I thought, Yes, Jesus did point the way to the understanding I was seeking. The man beside me was helping me also. Belief alone, surely, could not be enough. People believed for centuries that the world is flat, but their belief didn't make it so. Yet belief is a way of *opening* oneself to whatever truth there is, by turning one's thoughts expectantly in the right direction.

Yes, I then thought, but how do I know the direction itself is right? If all my expectations point in the wrong direction, I'm setting myself up for a great disillusionment.

Still, I then reflected, we don't live in a vacuum. Others have lived before us. Many of them have proved in their own lives which ways are successful, and which are not. Even to that fact, however, came an objection: Their successes, and their satisfactions, were to me vicarious. How could I know whether my own successes and satisfactions would be the same? No, I must probe deeper.

I told myself: I can believe only one thing in life: I want satisfaction. No, that's not enough (I corrected myself): I want *happiness*. And what is happiness? Is it a thing? No, it can't be, because what seems to give happiness to some people—a new car, for example—may be only a burden to me. Happiness, then, is a state of mind, not an object. All right, I want that state of mind. This means, then, that if all my belief flows in that direction, I'm open to whatever God gives me of *that* perfection. But if I hold back a single thought from that expectation, it will mean I've partially closed the curtain of my mind to His grace.

Then, *yes!* to this extent, belief *is* important! We have to hold high the banner of belief, to rally all our subconscious troops and get them to move in only one direction.

Suddenly, I felt like cheering my companion for what I would once have thought his all-too-narrow beliefs!

We turned into a driveway. The house before us was a comfortable size: neither too large nor too small. There was a little garden in front of it, with a few beds of smiling tulips. Before we could reach the house, the front door opened and a rather stout, middle-aged woman came out with a smile on her lips.

"Honey, you're back!" She said. "I'm so glad you made it in

time to welcome the children back from school. But—who is this?" She turned to me.

"This," John said, "is Beth Bentley. My wife. Sugar," he said to her, "he doesn't remember his name!"

"I didn't say that," I objected. "I said I want to forget my name."

"Well," said John, smiling good-humoredly, "we have to call him *something*! I've just been calling him, Friend. Will that do?" he asked me.

"Perfectly," I answered. "That's what I feel I am."

"Well Honey, well Friend," said Beth, "come right on in. I'll put a kettle on the stove. Would you like some tea?"

We both agreed. Before we could enter, however, a large dog came up the driveway and sniffed at me as if wondering where I'd come from.

"Oh, Rupert! Stop being so nosy!" Looking up at me apologetically, she finished, "He belongs to the people next door. They're Catholics!" This last remark contained a slight suggestion of disdain.

We went inside.

The living room was small, but cozy. Mrs. Bentley, with a comfortable motherly smile, offered me an arm chair and went into the kitchen to prepare tea. John seated himself in another chair, halfway facing me.

"Now," he said with a grin, "I can see better what you look like! Your search interests me. I've never met anyone before who *traveled* to find understanding. What's it like? I mean, what's it all about? I can see you traveling to find a job, or an address, or—gee, maybe a gold mine. But to find *understanding*! You won't find that either here or there."

"I know. Jesus said, 'Neither shall they say, Lo here! or, lo there! for, behold, the kingdom of God is within you.' But it seems to me the one great obstacle I face is myself! I'm traveling to shake off the consciousness of self-identity."

"What on earth for? I have a friend who insists the secret of success is self-esteem!"

"I have a strong feeling," I said with a smile, "that he's wrong."

At this juncture, however, Mrs. Bentley entered the room with a tray bearing two cups of hot water, with tea bags steeping in them. She set the tray down decisively on a little coffee table before us, then stood up with what looked like the battle light in her eyes. Firmly, like a judge pronouncing sentence, she declared, "I overheard you. It's perfectly obvious what Jesus meant by that saying. He didn't mean *you*, individually. He meant *you*, collectively. What he was saying was, 'Stop running around, and go to church!'"

"Churches didn't even exist, then," I reminded her. I just couldn't resist this little dig! She seemed so sure of herself.

"Well," she declared firmly, "there were worshipers, and he was addressing them. He spoke to groups of worshipers, moreover. He was saying that the kingdom of God is wherever worshipers gather together. He also said, 'Where two or three are gathered together in my name, there am I in the midst of them.' Matthew 18:20."

"And you say therefore you've already found the kingdom of God in your own church?"

"Well, certainly!"

"How would you define this kingdom, then? What makes it godly? Does perfection thrive there?"

"Well, of course, people are people. You can't ask for perfection of them. But they're a lot better than those Catholics next door!"

"What makes them better?"

"Well, they go to church—the *true* church. They haven't let themselves be sucked in by all those popish practices."

"Do you know what those practices are?"

"No, and I don't want to know."

Well, I'm not a Catholic, but I wasn't going to add to my self-definitions by calling myself a "non-Catholic"! I wanted to leave *all* self-definitions behind me. My instant reaction was a wish to resist her intolerance. But then I thought, "No. Reaction isn't the way." I had read years ago about a man who was beaten back repeatedly to shore by the ocean waves. Rising one more time to his knees, he had seen a fragile seashell tumbling in the surf beside him. He noticed that, though fragile, it was still intact: it had flowed *with* the currents!

And then I reflected, I'm on a quest for understanding. This must mean, also, for *self*-understanding. If I react to her intolerance, I will in a sense be trying to push it out of my own life. By resistance, I'll only create tension in myself. Why not try, instead, to go *with* the flow? It's not that I must agree with her, but maybe I can rechannel her energy. I decided to try humor.

With a smile, I said, "Do you like cockroaches?"

She had inhaled as if on the point of launching into a diatribe. My question brought her up short.

"Cockroaches?" she asked after a pause. "What have cockroaches to do with anything?"

"Just tell me; I'm curious. Do you like cockroaches?"

She laughed. "Well, I can't really say that I do. Does anyone?"

"But aren't cockroaches God's creatures? Do you love God?"

"Well, of course I do!"

"Do you love Him, but dislike what He does?"

She laughed. "Well, if I stand back a little I guess I can enjoy His variety in producing *even* cockroaches!"

"Then what about Catholics?"

"Well," she chuckled, "I guess I can like them in that sense, also!"

"Do your neighbors enjoy the same things you do?"

"Mostly the same things, I suppose."

"Do they speak the same language you do?"

"Well, of course. We're Americans."

"They speak it better than any cockroach can, right?"

She laughed again. "Oh, you're a wily one! Of course, they're like us in most respects. We just disagree on doctrine."

"So you love mankind. It's only people you can't stand, right?"

She seemed to relax. "That's about it, I guess. Jesus taught us to love our neighbor. Maybe I can allow those Catholics next door a little of the free air I breathe!" She resumed her first kind, motherly appearance and sat down with a smile.

John commented, "People say comparisons are odious, but without them, how can we ever learn discrimination?"

And I said, "I think we must see that, in the realm of ideas, distinctions exist, and can be important. Beneath those ideas, however, the consciousness that gave rise to them is the same. It is that consciousness we should embrace, not its specific manifestations. That is to say, we should love God in everything, and in everyone, even when we disagree with the specific things people do. We should dismiss the sin, but not the sinner, for the sinner, at least, has the potential to turn away from sin."

John looked at me wide-eyed. "That means—hell may exist, but no one can be condemned to remain there eternally!"

"Why, John! What are you saying?" his wife asked.

I said to her, "If your own son were to be condemned to hell, wouldn't you feel badly for him?"

"Well, of course!"

"I mean, wouldn't you feel there was *some* goodness in him, some potential of which he was being deprived?"

"How could I not? There's a lot of goodness in that boy, even if he does get into a bit of mischief sometimes!"

"And don't you think God loves him, in spite of his mischief?"

"Well, of course He does! He loves us all."

"Then, loving us, can't He distinguish between what we do and what we *are*?"

"I see that you're right," she concluded pensively. "I'm afraid I get carried away a little sometimes by my own feelings. Jesus taught us to love everybody. Now I see that I can love others, even if I disagree with them. Thank you! Tolerance, with no lessening of discrimination. This makes me feel much more relaxed, inside. Yes, I like it!"

Just then there came a loud knock on the door.

"May I come in?" a boisterous voice cried. "It's Bob."

"Bob Yates!" said John with a smile. "Speak of the devil, and here he is! It's the man I told you about, who says that success requires self-esteem. Not quite your philosophy! Come in," he then called.

A large man burst in, all smiles and good fellowship.

"Hi! I was driving by, and just thought I'd give you folks a treat. Glad to see me?"

"Why sure, Bob," said Mrs. Bentley with a kindly smile. "What've you been doing lately? Giving all the girls the benefit of your manly presence?"

"Ha, ha! Well, ya know, what you don't spread around just goes to waste! Hey, listen! I've just come up with a red hot idea. Talk about think tanks: that's me! You know what the pastor's been saying, about wantin' more people to hear the Word of God? Well, what about havin' a truck, with a loudspeaker pointing in all directions, drive around town Sunday mornings and give the message: 'It's Sunday morning! Get fired up by a good sermon! Don't be fried in the fires of hell!' Doesn't that sound great?" He looked at us beaming, anticipating our enthusiastic approval.

John said, "Well Bob, it's—an idea. I mean, people will get the message. But do you think everyone will appreciate all this promotion on their day of rest? Doesn't the Bible recommend a day of rest?"

"Rest, yes, but not from the Word of God!"

I said, "This sounds rather like self-promotion."

"So what's wrong with that?"

"Do you think God likes it when we try to make ourselves so all-important?"

"Why, sure. The bigger we are, the bigger we make God

look. People look up to you, if you're important. And if you're representing God, they look up to Him even more. The bigger the man, the bigger the firm looks he represents. Self-importance is the first step to becoming great in this man's world. What I always say is, Blow your own trumpet; no one else will ever blow it so well. Ha, ha!"

"Humility, however, is a Christian virtue."

"Ha, ha! I bet people say that just to eliminate the competition!"

"The thing is, where does your power come from?"

"Well, obviously, it comes from *me* if I have the guts to claim it. What it takes to get ahead in life is *guts*! Winning isn't for the weak."

"Granted," I said, "but am I the source of power, or am I a channel for it? You're denying God Himself, if you consider yourself that source."

"Philosophy! Bah! I could never stomach all that heavy stuff. Just give me the opportunity to shine, and I'll shine with the best of 'em. Better still, I'll *make* that opportunity!"

"And your little star will twinkle on through the night, needing a telescope even to be seen!"

"Ah, nuts to all that! Well, gotta be goin'. S'long, John. Be seein' ya, Beth." And out he went like a candle. That was Bob Yates.

I said afterward, "It isn't only that we can understand better, and accomplish more, when we call on God's power, but ego poses the supreme barrier to our very awareness of God's presence."

"But what *is* any such awareness, really?" asked Mrs. Bentley. "I mean, He's up in heaven. We're down here on earth. We're separated by vast distances. He watches us always, but we're on our own down here, doing our best, but waiting for Judgment Day."

"How do you suppose He made us all? Is He like a potter molding clay? If so, where did He get the clay?"

"He just—well, I don't know—produced it. Produced us."

"Like magic?"

"Yes, I guess you could say that."

"But something can't come out of nothing. Even magic can't do that. All it can produce is illusions."

"But *I'm* no illusion! I pinch my hand, and see? It hurts."

"There is self-awareness there. And there is feeling. These two are the fundamental realities: self-awareness, and feeling. But your body is not the *source* of that self-awareness. It takes awareness to know that you even exist. Thinking can't *produce* that knowledge; you need the awareness, first, to be able even to think. And feeling can't be produced by analysis: it, too, simply is. It's how we direct it that makes it either real or illusory. In a nightmare you may see appalling scenes that, after you wake up, make you laugh. The scenes were illusory. The feelings were illusory. But the *ability* to feel, and to feel terrified, was real for all that. That ability to feel, and that awareness of a self that could be threatened— these are the abiding realities."

"Good heavens! I never thought of it that way. I think you're saying also, the kingdom of God isn't in church. His kingdom isn't a place, or a *thing*. Maybe you're right. Maybe Jesus did mean we should seek actual contact with him, and not just believe in him. But I don't understand. *How* can I open myself to that contact? Where is he? Heaven, we know, is up there somewhere. But will I be closer to him if I stand on a high hill?"

"Here," I said, "is why Jesus told us the kingdom of God is within you. All the real work is on our own selves, on improving and—yes, literally—raising our own consciousness. When we think *upward* we are happier, more prone to success, and better able to do everything. Even in a slum, we can be closer to heaven in our own thoughts. But when we think *downward*, our minds become clouded and heavy; a sort of mental darkness prevents us from doing anything well; and we aren't happy. Even among beautiful scenes we feel out of sympathy with beauty. Heaven does lie within us. And the more we lift up our hearts to the Lord, the better He can fill our cups. Moreover, if the cup is empty of self-seeking, He can fill it with His divine nectar of bliss."

"Wow! You should have been a poet." She smiled. "So we should empty ourselves so that He can fill us. I like that! But how, exactly, can we go about doing that? I've tried mentally groveling before Him, and I find all I think about is how small I am. I don't think about Him."

"Yes, that's what happens. I think we must just forget ourselves. Say, 'You please do this, Lord, through me.' In that way, we'll attract more of His inspiration and power."

John broke in then, "This means that, in addition to calling on the Lord, we should listen for His answer."

"Yes. And that means listening in silence. He can only speak to us if we will shut up!"

"You mean—meditating! I've heard of that, but I've never done it. I thought it was a heathen practice."

"Yet Jesus went into the wilderness to be alone with God."

"That was Jesus. His case was different."

"No, I think he came on earth to show us what we, too, can be and do. He himself said that."

"Well, glory be! I don't know what to think any more. Maybe the important thing in religion is not what we believe, but what we practice and experience for ourselves. Maybe knowledge itself is the fruit of experience, not of belief."

"I myself think so," I said. "But I'm grateful to you for showing me the importance of believing, too, as a prior condition for true commitment. And I'm grateful to you both for showing me that intolerance can be a stepping stone to greater wisdom, for at least it shows a willingness to see that there are rights and wrongs."

"Friend," said Mrs. Bentley, "I like you. Have you anywhere to sleep for tonight?"

"So far I haven't any."

"We have a spare bedroom. Would you like to spend the night here?"

"I'd be very grateful," I said.

And so the first leg of my journey ended—and ended well, I thought. I'd learned from it, and I'd grown through it by helping others. I was richer in my own understanding.

THREE

The Children
Come Home

W ITH A BANG THE DOOR OPENED.
"We're home!" two young voices called out even as they came inside. Then it was like an invasion—a wave suddenly hitting a pier, or a clanking jalopy suddenly coming to a halt at a stop light—they saw us assembled in the living room, and paused. I saw there a small boy, and an even smaller girl.

"Oh, hi!" they said more quietly as they entered the room. "Sorry," said the boy. "We didn't expect to find you all so nearby."

The little girl came running over to Beth Bentley. "Mommy, I can write!"

"That's wonderful, dear. You must show me how well you do it. But first I'd like you to meet our visitor." Turning to me, she said, "This is little Jenny. She's six years old. And this is Ben; he's ten." To the children she said, "We call this gentleman, Friend."

"Hullo, Mr. Friend," said Ben gravely.

"Hello, Mister," said Jenny.

"'Ben, he's ten,'" said Ben with a giggle. "I like that! It rhymes."

"Mommy, here's a pencil. Give me a piece of paper and I'll show you what I can do!"

Mrs. Bentley picked up a piece of notepaper from the coffee table and gave it to her daughter. The little girl carefully and elaborately wrote out the words: "I see you."

"Why, that's marvelous!" cried her mother.

"Well done, Jenny!" said her father.

"What do you think?" said Mrs. Bentley, turning to me. "This is an important moment in her life."

"Soon she'll be writing novels!" I said with a smile. And then—realizing that with children you can't expect them to enter your world; you have to enter theirs—I said, "I learned something else when I was your age that I bet you don't know."

"What?" asked Jenny a little skeptically.

"I learned that I can go through a keyhole!"

"A keyhole! You're kidding!"

"No, I'm not. And I can teach you how to go through one, too."

"Come on!" she challenged with a doubtful grin. "Show me!"

I wrote the letter "I" on a torn-off piece of the note paper, got up and pushed it through the keyhole of the nearest door.

"That's cheating!" Jenny giggled.

"No it's not. I did just what I said I could do. And you can do it too. Just write the letter 'U,' and do the same!"

"Oh, this is fun! I'll have to do it for my friends at school! But in that case the 'U' wouldn't be 'I.'"

"True enough. And who is either of those two? Please just tell me something."

"What?"

"Why aren't you that '*I*' on a piece of paper? Why are you, you?"

"That's a silly question!"

"It seems it, I know. But it's something I keep asking myself: Who am I, really?"

"Why, don't you *know*?"

"I just wonder."

"Well, I know who *I* am. I'm Jenny, and I'm six."

"Yes, Jenny," I conceded, "that's who you are for now. But someday you'll be seven. And then some day, many years from now, you'll be eighty-seven. But you'll still be Jenny. And you'll still be the same person. Yet you'll also be different. Who is Jenny, really?"

And I thought of my wife. Who is she now? I asked myself. Where is she? She must have another name. What, in her, is the constant and changeless reality?

"I like being a little child," Jenny declared. "I can crawl into little places, where no one can find me!"

"Yes, of course, Jenny." To Mrs. Bentley I said, "Please forgive me for catechizing her like this."

"That's all right. You run off and play now, Jenny." To me she then said, "You were catechizing me, too. But I've read a little Shakespeare. I guess we all play our little roles in life. I'm a mother; she's a child; John's in business. Is that all we are? You say that Jesus came to show us we can be like him. I wonder what that means, exactly."

But John had something else on his mind.

"Ben," he said, "you've been awfully quiet. Is something bothering you?"

"Yeah, it's Tom Yates. He's a bully."

John turned to me. "That's Bob Yates's boy. Wouldn't you know it!" Then he asked Ben, "What's he been doing to you, son?"

"He pushed me as we were going into a classroom. I pushed him back, and he said, 'Boy, am I going to get *you*!' I know he means it, Dad."

"Like father, like son," said John musingly.

"Tom's much bigger 'n I am," said Ben.

I hazarded a thought: "Why not try taking lessons from Mother Nature? In the animal kingdom, some of the smaller animals have evolved very creative methods of self-defense. Think of the skunk! Maybe you could get a peculiar scent at a gardening shop; put it into a little perfume spray bottle, then release little spurts of that scent around you whenever Tom comes near. Don't spray *him* with it; he'd only take the bottle from you. But you could spray the air right around you."

Ben laughed. "Well, but maybe I wouldn't like that scent either!"

"Would you like a beating more?"

"Well," he conceded with a grin, "maybe not!"

"And here's another thing you might try. You know about

porcupines. Maybe your mother could sew pins onto a double cloth, with a string attached. The next time Tommy tries to shoulder you, you could pull down on the string and make those pins stand out straight. I bet he'd quickly get the message that it was better not to mess with you. Often, with bullies, all you need is to convey the message: 'Go mess with someone else.'"

At this thought, Ben laughed delightedly. "Oh, mom, do you think you could do that?"

His mother smiled with amusement, and said, "I'd be glad to try. I certainly don't like his menacing you like that."

"But here's something else you can do," I said. "In life, it's important not to be a doormat for anyone. In the Himalayas there's a little black bear which tigers usually avoid, because the bears stand up to them. Bullies are like dogs: When they see something running away from them, they give chase. Have you ever seen a dog run after a moving car? It's simple dog psychology. When a bully, too, sees that you're afraid of him, your fear arouses his aggressive instincts. Don't threaten him; and don't oppose him. Just look at him firmly; let him know you're not afraid of him."

Ben said, "That's fine. But I *am* afraid! I don't want to be beaten up by him."

"Then work on yourself. Work on your attitude. You'll find that, if you can be centered in yourself and not react emotionally, his hostility toward you will evaporate. Wish him well! You might even find some subject on which you can ask his advice.

"The main thing," I continued, "is to *respect* everyone. When you respect others, they will respect you. We need to learn how not to wish harm to anyone. The way to do that is to offer everyone your sincere respect."

"But how can I respect stupidity? How can I respect ignorance, and people who hold silly ideas?"

"Well, you can respect their right to be stupid! their right to be as ignorant as they choose. Everybody has a right to come to understanding at his own speed. You can even make a game of it: 'Let me see just how creatively stupid this person can be.' Then tell yourself, 'This person is, in his own way, a real athlete!'"

Ben giggled. "I like that!" he cried. "So I can respect his ignorance just for being so colossal. Yes, I like that!"

"But there's another thing I've learned. If there's anything I'm afraid of, I make a practice of imagining it really happening. And then I ask myself, 'All right, what now?' People always seem able to carry on, somehow, whatever happens to them. In this way, I find I can even bear pain without letting it bother me. I tell myself a little pain never hurt anyone! We must learn how to go through life untouched by anything that happens."

"I can't follow you there!" he exclaimed.

"No, I guess it's something I'm working on in myself. I've lost . . . Well, I won't bother you with that."

"But you've helped all of us," protested Mrs. Bentley, smiling with sympathy. "If we can do anything for you, I hope you'll give us the chance."

"Well," I answered her, "I've just lost my wife. She was very dear to me, but now she's dead, and I'm trying to reconcile myself to living without her."

"Well, let's hope she safe and snug in the arms of Jesus."

"My wife," I replied, "was Jewish."

"Oh."

John said, "Then how come you . . . ?"

Mrs. Bentley broke in with, "I once met a Jewish woman at the Johnsons. What I remember about her is that she was nice and clean!"

Tactfully changing the subject, Ben remarked, "I often see the forms of faces in our carpet. In fact, wherever I look, if there are abstract patterns I see faces in them. How come?"

"Well, for one thing, certainly," I said, "it shows you have a creative imagination."

"You do have that, Ben!" his mother commented.

"Yes," John added. "But seeing things that aren't there can't be good!"

"Still," I remarked, "Jesus Christ said, 'Suffer little children to come unto me, for of such is the kingdom of heaven.'"

John said smiling, "Suffer! Sometimes that about sums it up!"

Mrs. Bentley remarked, "But our Bible translates the expression differently: 'Let little children. . . .'"

"Anyway," I continued, "one thing I think Jesus meant was that children have the capacity to see things afresh, without prior conditioning. Obviously he didn't mean that to be worthy of heaven we should become *childish!*"

"The thing is, though," Ben commented, "the images I see are all caricatures. None of them are normal, and certainly none of them are beautiful."

"And there," I said, "I think the word 'childlike' doesn't work so well. To my mind, to be childlike means to see things without prior conditioning. But if we see things in caricature, it means we have images formed in our minds already, exaggerating and distorting reality. Surely, then, these are all images of delusion—of what isn't really there. Shouldn't imagination itself give us possibilities of things that might indeed be there?"

"I think you're right," said John. "But then, apart from caricatures, if we accept the possibility of alternative realities, it seems to me we'll be more likely to choose correctly."

"Dogmatism, then," I went on, "is the opposite of childlike. It limits one to a single, fixed reality. It isn't at all similar to what Jesus described as the kingdom of heaven."

"I guess that's right," John answered thoughtfully.

"And the more we can approach truth openly, without prejudice, and don't box it in with too much reasoning, the more likely we are to *experience* it."

"Well, I hadn't really thought of experiencing truth. To me, it has just been something to believe in."

Mrs. Bentley broke in at this point to say, "Our pastor and his wife are coming to dinner tonight. I think you'll enjoy talking with them."

"Will he ever!" said John with a chuckle. "Whatever happens, I think *we'll* have fun."

"They should be here soon," said Mrs. Bentley with a smile.

FOUR

The Believers

T HE PASTOR AND HIS WIFE ARRIVED.
      "Hello, Susan," boomed the pastor. "Hello John."
"Welcome, Pastor Cooper," the Bryants said. "We'd like
to present our guest to you. We know him only as Friend."

"Greetings, Friend!" I said with a welcoming smile.

"Well met!" they both exclaimed. "It's always a pleasure to
greet fellow believers."

"Well, we think he's a believer," said Susan, "but we're not
completely sure. Anyway, we've gained a lot from his company. He's very eloquent."

Pastor Cooper shook hands with me, but looked at me
appraisingly as if sniffing competition.

"Well, we'll talk about that later," he said. "Shall we sit
down a bit in the living room?"

"Do," said John. "Take your usual armchair." It was the
chair I'd been sitting in, but I surrendered it to him readily.

There followed some chitchat. Pastor Cooper was interested in Ben's problems with the bully, and then in the conversation they'd had about patterns on the carpet.

"Yes, I can see something interesting in what you said, Friend, about dogmatism. But we folks like to think we don't preach dogmas: we preach truths."

"What truths do you preach?" I inquired, interested.

"Well, for one thing we preach that infant baptism is a mistake. Unless and until one has reached the age of consent, how can baptizing him be effective?"

"I certainly agree with you that it isn't enough for the parents to give their child to God. The child, too, must give its consent. Still, I suppose it helps at least to offer it to God. One is more likely, then, to raise it in godly ways."

"Oh, I suppose there can't be any real harm in it. But to become one of God's elect, we must give our wholehearted consent to become his own. We also believe, therefore, in total immersion at baptism. One's whole body needs to be bathed in the baptismal waters. It isn't enough only to be sprinkled at the font."

"I see," said, not wishing to argue.

"Let me ask you: Have you been baptized?"

"Well, I was baptized at birth, which you tell me doesn't count. And then I was confirmed at the age of thirteen, which means I gave full consent to the prior fact of my baptism. And even then I wasn't old enough to discriminate clearly!"

"I'd call that a double blasphemy: To baptize you before you're old enough to consent, and confirm that baptism before you're mature enough even to drive, or to vote! You'd better get yourself baptized right, Brother, or you're going to go to hell!"

"But what will baptism do? So I get a good bath, and believe I'm being cleansed by the waters of Spirit. What in me, specifically, will be cleansed?"

"Why, your soul, Friend! Your sins will all be washed away."

"Do you mean that if I committed the sin of doing down a neighbor in a sale, he will forgive me that sin if I get baptized?"

"Well, your neighbor may not forgive you, but God will forgive you."

"And does baptism guarantee I won't cheat anyone else ever again?"

"Well, no, it doesn't guarantee present perfection, but it does guarantee God's forgiveness, through Jesus Christ."

"In other words, baptism is my passport to keep right on sinning?"

"Well no," Pastor Cooper acknowledged with a slightly disgruntled look. "One must also try not to sin again."

"But does baptism make one more likely to succeed in that effort?"

"Well, it does, if one truly believes."

"But what if a non-formal—that it to say, a non-churchgoing Christian—believes in Christ, and does his best to live a good life: Can we say of him that, because he isn't baptized, he fails to attract Christ's blessings?"

"Baptism is a sacrament. If one believes, and tries, he should certainly want to be baptized also."

"Okay, but what if he doesn't even know about this teaching? Is there a hope for him?"

"Poor fellow, then he goes to hell."

"And you're telling me God loves us all, but He gives some people a chance to be saved, and others no chance at all?"

"Well, God's will is inscrutable. Who are we to question it?"

"I should think, since He gave us intelligence, he must *want* us to question it! How else can we arrive at understanding?"

"All Jesus asks of us is that we believe."

"Yet Proverbs tells us, 'In all thy getting, get understanding.' You quoted those words to me in the car, John. Remember?"

"Yes, Proverbs 4:7," cut in Pastor Cooper. "But all the understanding we Christians need is to know that Jesus died for our sins. If we accept him in our hearts, he will assume our sins, and we shall be saved."

At this point, Beth Bentley called us to the table. The rest of the conversation continued as we passed dishes around and ate her sumptuous repast.

"You said," I resumed around a mouthful of potato, "that he will assume our sins if we accept him. But in this scientific age, we've learned to demand proofs. Let's say someone was a drunkard before his conversion. Let's say even that conversion stopped him from drinking. Would you say that sin of drunkenness had been wiped out by his belief?"

"Yes, most certainly," the pastor replied.

"Supposing, during his years of drunkenness, he had beaten someone up. I asked you this question before, in the context of cheating. Do you believe that person would now forgive you?"

"Well, that would depend on the person."

"Exactly. Jesus may have forgiven him, but in this world he would still have to face the consequences of his sin. So, then, in what sense would he really be forgiven? Would it be only that he wouldn't have to pay after death?"

"That's right. He wouldn't go to hell."

"But it seems to me to be asking a good deal to believe that I'll be forgiven after death, when I see no signs of such forgiveness here on earth. Does baptism at least change one in his outward demeanor?"

"Well—yes! He goes to church. He sings to God."

"And he may continue to cheat his neighbor. He may still get angry. It seems to me," I said, "that baptism isn't the final answer."

"Well, I grant you a person may continue sinning. After all, who is perfect, except God?"

"Yet Jesus said, 'Be ye therefore perfect, even as your father in heaven is perfect.'"

"Yes. Some translations say 'good,' or 'transformed.' But yes, the Bible does say substantially that."

"So then, that passage has to mean that God wants us to achieve perfection here on earth, and not have it simply handed to us after death, provided we've gone through the prescribed rituals, like baptism, beforehand."

"Well, Friend, I'm not trying to rewrite the Bible! It's all plainly stated there. Many people claim that Jesus was not God, and for that matter that he never claimed to be God. Is that True? No, it is not. In Isaiah 53:3–6, it says of the coming Messiah, 'He was despised and rejected by men, a man of sorrows, and familiar with suffering. . . . He was despised, and we esteemed him not. Surely he took up our infirmities and carried our sorrow, yet we considered him stricken by God, smitten by him, and afflicted. But he was pierced for our transgressions, he was crushed for our iniquities; the punishment that brought us peace was upon him, and by his wounds we are healed. We all, like sheep, have gone astray, each of us has turned to his own way; and the LORD has laid on him the iniquity of us all.'"

"Well, that's scripture and I won't argue with it," I said. "But I can't help questioning this interpretation of it. Quotations alone don't suffice: we must also understand their meaning correctly. That, to me, is the disadvantage of making the Bible your sole authority."

"So then, how do you interpret that saying?"

"Well, I interpret it as meaning Christ will bear all our iniquities, or sins. That's fine, except it goes against what I actually see happening all around me. People do seem to 'bear the marks of their own iniquity.' A drunkard becomes fuzzy in his thinking. An avaricious man shows his greed for money and possessions in his puffy cheeks, his hungry eyes, his loud voice. A proud man shows his pride in the very way he looks down his nose at the world. And yet, such persons may be believing Christians. I think there's more to it than baptism. We can't just be the passive recipients of grace. We must also be active in our own redemption. When Jesus said, 'Be ye therefore perfect,' he was telling us to do our part also in the process. That is why he gave that as a commandment, rather than as a mere prediction."

"The American Standard version says, 'Ye therefore shall be perfect, as your heavenly Father is. . . .' So it seems to be a matter of translation, too. In this version, God and Jesus do all the work."

"Are you saying, then," I asked, "that we shouldn't even try to be good?"

"Basically I'm saying that in God's eyes we are all sinners. St. Paul said, 'Lest any man should boast.' For true believers, everything comes by grace alone."

"Very well, but let me give you an analogy. Think of grace as the sunlight on the side of a building. If a certain room in that building has its curtains drawn shut, the sunlight of grace won't be able to enter in." Turning to John, I reminded him, "I gave you that example earlier."

"That's right, you did," John said, but he wasn't smiling. This conversation was completely absorbing his attention.

"All right then," I continued, "let's say that opening the curtains means to believe in Christ and accept him. That much self-effort St. Paul himself grants us as being necessary."

"Well, I'll accept your point, provisionally."

I went on, "But Jesus said also, 'Blessed are the pure in heart, for they shall see God.' What, to your mind, constitutes purity of heart?"

"I say that purity of heart means to accept Christ."

"Doesn't it also mean not to hate anyone?"

"Well, truly to love Christ means also, of course, not to hate anyone."

"Good. But then, are all of your parishioners free from hatred?"

"Well, we are all sinners."

"How can you be, if Jesus has taken away all your sins?"

"All right, I grant you that perfection is not for this world."

"How can we be sure it's for the next world? And back to the question about purity of heart, doesn't such purity also mean to be without pride, and anger, and jealousy, and the slightest desire to get even for past hurts?"

"Well, yes, I suppose it must."

"Then was Jesus holding out an impossible ideal when he told us to be pure in heart?"

"But he wasn't actually telling us to be *that* perfect! He was just holding out an ideal."

"And didn't he also imply that we should work toward achieving that ideal?"

"Well, yes, of course he did. But he knew we are all sinners. He just . . ." Pastor Cooper paused in some perplexity.

"Yes? Doesn't it seem to you that calling oneself a sinner gives one a good excuse to go right on sinning?"

"Well," he laughed. "But at the same time, it's always good to be humble."

"Humble, yes, but why should we abase ourselves needlessly?"

"No? What, then, is humility in your eyes?"

"I see it" I said, "as meaning that we see God alone, in everything, as the true Doer. We don't have to say that everything we do and are is bad!"

"And what of our wrong deeds? Isn't it safer to accept that *nothing* we can do has any merit in God's eyes at all?"

"I don't think," I replied, "that it really has any merit anyway. He loves us not for what we do, but for what we are: His children."

"Oh, I think you altogether mistake His charity towards us. God hates sin! In His eyes, we are an abomination!"

"The picture you paint of His creation and its creatures is certainly bleak!"

"We are creatures of original sin—the descendants of Adam and Eve. And you, I am sad to say, will spend eternity in hell if you don't reform your views!"

"And can you really believe," I expostulated, but with a smile (after all, the picture he painted of my future destiny was more or a general caricature than a personal malediction!), "that for a few years spent in ignorance, God will want me to suffer through all eternity? You make me think of that vengeful God behind the altar in the Sistine chapel, whose entire energy seems directed in condemnation of the poor damned!"

Pastor Cooper wiped his brow. We were now having dessert, but it didn't seem to taste very sweet to him. He frowned heavily.

"I don't want to make heavy weather here this evening," he said. "We're pretty liberal in our church. We allow considerable latitude of belief in our different congregations. But I must say, Stranger, you hold some pretty dangerous ideas in that head of yours."

"Dangerous to me? Or dangerous to those who hold different beliefs? And in the latter case, is it the truth that is dangerous? I've only suggested that the Christian saying is true: 'God helps those who help themselves.' I've suggested we try also to improve ourselves—that we work as much as possible to achieve purity of heart by our own efforts, also.

And I'm suggesting that Jesus wanted us at least to *strive* toward perfection. I haven't said that there isn't an absolute need for grace. I've said only that we should keep our minds open to receive it."

"Well, in all this I'm forced to agree with you. But don't you think we show our openness to his grace by accepting baptism?"

"As regards baptism, isn't it important also that we accept baptism with complete openness and surrender of heart?"

"Yes, of course that's important."

"Then wouldn't you also say that many, or even most, people who call themselves Christians probably have not accepted even baptism in wholly the right spirit, and are therefore not fully baptized?"

"Well, look, you're going too far!"

"But I'm saying that an *attitude* of perfect surrender is more important than baptism itself."

"No, I won't accept that one can be saved without baptism."

"And you won't accept that, if a person isn't baptized, he doesn't necessarily go to hell?"

"Well, *of course* he goes to hell. The Bible says so!"

"Jesus said, 'Blessed are the pure in heart, for they shall see God.' He didn't even say, 'Blessed are my followers.' He was speaking of a principle, not of an outward affiliation."

"Well, the affiliation was implied!"

"What about Jews, if they are pure in heart as we've defined purity? Or Hindus? Or Buddhists? Or Muslims? And what about all the thousands who lived and died before Jesus was even born?"

"Look, the truth is hard, and it isn't easy to accept it, but it's a fact that the Bible tells us only those who accept Jesus Christ shall be saved!" The good pastor had become somewhat heated by this time, and seemed on the verge of losing his temper. So I said to him, "Well, I may get to hell by and by, but I don't want to see you burning there already—with anger! Let's just say that I do believe in God, and in Jesus Christ. My way to him may be different from yours, but can't we accept that our different trails lead to the same summit?"

"Yes," Pastor Cooper said, after a long-drawn inhalation conceding the point. To his hostess he said, "I'm not sure it's safe to have this man in your home. I don't altogether approve of all his ideas." To me then he said, "Just what are you looking for, Friend?"

"I'm on a quest for understanding."

"Well, if so, I hope you've gained a little from our discussion?"

"I have," I replied. "I've understood that ideas can become as fixed as screws in a board. I've learned to offer up every idea I have in my own head to divine wisdom: to ask of life and of God, always, 'What is the truth?'"

"Well, we have the answer to that question, but you won't accept it."

"What I think you have is a way station. It's like using a pick when climbing a mountain: driving the pick firmly into the cliff above one, to hoist oneself another notch higher. But I think your own understanding will show you, in time, that you've still a distance to climb."

"I can't accept that. What's true is true."

"And I won't argue, though I think you'll find in time that our understanding of truth itself, in this world of relativities, can become refined."

He laughed as his wife and he rose from the table. "Well, I appreciate hearing your point of view on these things."

His wife added, "Perhaps you'd like to come to our church this Sunday."

"It's kind of you to invite me. But I'm on a long pilgrimage. I must be on my way tomorrow."

"Well, we wish you all blessings!" The two of them smiled before changing the subject, and passing on to small talk.

I was grateful for this encounter. For one thing, it helped me in my quest by showing me the importance—indeed, the necessity—for thinking things out for myself.

FIVE

An Atheist

T HE FOLLOWING MORNING I BREAKFASTED WITH the whole family. We smiled at one another. After breakfast, the children went off to school, and John went off to work.

"I'll tell my schoolmates I can go through a keyhole!" cried Jenny enthusiastically.

"And I'll ask Tom Yates," Ben cried, "if he can help me understand what Jesus meant when he said we should all be like children. That should make him think a bit! He thinks he's so grown-up and important."

I had no particular schedule, and was therefore the last to leave. As I said goodbye, Beth shook me gratefully by the hand.

"Friend," she said, "you have helped us to see life as a pilgrimage to perfection. Thank you so much for that!"

"And I, too, am grateful, Beth. This visit has advanced me in my own quest for understanding. I see more deeply, now, that people are more than their beliefs: that all of us are souls, and much more than human beings. The truth, for all of us, lies beyond any definition we can create of it. Meeting all of you has helped to confirm me in my insight that this quest of mine is really a quest for *self*-understanding. Thank you."

I set off gladly down the road with a song on my lips. The song had lyrics, of which I give here the first stanza:

There's joy in the heavens,
A smile on the mountains,
And melody sings everywhere!
The flowers are all laughing
To welcome the morning:
Your soul is as free as the air.

Birds were singing in the trees, and sunlight, like blood through the body, was warming the whole countryside. A gentle breeze played over the meadow grass by the road, and gay flowers nodded and smiled at me as I walked along. There was a spring in my step, and I wondered what new adventure awaited me today.

"Holy Mother," I prayed after enjoying the morning sunshine for a time, "send me some fresh experience today that will deepen my understanding in this quest of mine."

Just then a car stopped beside me, and a voice called out, "Would you like a ride?"

"Gladly," I said, and got in beside the driver. I found him a wizened old fellow of about sixty.

"Are you going far?" I asked him.

"Well, I'll stop at the next village," he replied. "Then I go on a bit farther. Where are you headed?"

"I'm on a personal quest," I said.

"That's an odd answer," was his comment. "What are you seeking?"

"I'm on a quest for understanding."

"Even odder, unless that's the name of a village! I'm not sure you'll ever find what you're seeking. Where are you coming from, that you should have this motivation?"

"I'm coming from ignorance as to who I really am."

"Why, it's surely simple enough to know who you are. Haven't you a name?"

"I'm trying to dissociate myself from it."

"Well, if you're starting from zero, I don't see how you can expect to progress anywhere at all."

"But I see my quest as a search for the God in me."

"The God in—now, that's a laugh! God is the biggest zero of them all!"

"I agree with you. He's nothing—that is to say, He is no thing."

"Oh, come now, surely you don't believe He really exists?"

"I do indeed. I *know* He exists."

"Why, science exploded that God myth centuries ago! Get with it! Your brain is just a computer. Someday we'll have intelligent computers campaigning for computer rights. Why, even now they can outthink human beings. Oh, well, here we are at the village. Care to come in with me for a cup of coffee?"

We went inside, where he ordered two cups of coffee and brought them over to a table. "Here we can talk a bit," he said. "By the way, my name's Isaac—as in Isaac Newton." He smiled wryly.

"And mine's—well, just Friend, as in Owl in the movie *Bambi*."

"Bambi! Is *that* your frame of reality? Hardly an auspicious point of departure for a discussion about God! Well then, Friend Owl, do you pretend that God is more than the myth Bambi was?"

"Well, let me answer you with another question: Do you really think we are only thinking machines?"

"Well, what else can we be? Descartes, after many years of pondering the subject of our existence, concluded, 'I think; therefore I am.' That is the decree of science, too. All we are is thinking machines—robots, if you will, made of flesh and blood."

"I'm sorry, but I don't will! No robot could be programmed to ask such questions as, 'What is the meaning of existence?' You couldn't program a robot to answer that question significantly, either. Nor could you expect it to answer, except very superficially, questions like, 'What is true happiness?' A robot could only equate happiness with something sensory."

"Oh, I don't know," said Isaac. "I mean, what else is happiness, really? In fact, does it even exist? Happiness is an emotion, and our emotions are only movements of energy passing through our nervous system."

"There are levels of feeling, however," I answered, "that are deeper than any emotion. They can't be programmed. Feeling itself can't be programmed: it just *is*. Your reasoned thinking has a mechanical aspect to it, but feeling doesn't. Feeling isn't the product of thinking at all. Look at the earthworm. I can't imagine it thinking. I can't imagine it having anything so complicated as an emotion. Yet if you

prick it with a pin, it will writhe away. That's because it has
feeling. It also has self-consciousness. Computers can outthink us in certain respects even now, but no computer can
ever think beyond the limits of its programming. There are
two things which science will never be able to create: feeling, and self-awareness. These two realities are inborn in us;
they aren't, and never can be, programmed."

"Well, but for a thing to be inborn also implies a sort of
programming: a programming from within."

"I wouldn't call that programming. I'd call it Being. The
truth is, it isn't because you think that you are conscious of
existing. Rather, you are able to think because you already
know that you exist. You are *conscious* of feeling, and of
existing."

"Well, I hadn't thought about that earthworm. You've a
point there. But science has proved to us that God doesn't
exist—that life itself has no purpose or meaning. Moral values are not absolute, but relative. In the great scheme of
things, it doesn't really matter what we do, since evil, as
such, doesn't even exist."

"If I say that God is a blue crocodile, and then, after
much research, find that there is no such crocodile, can I
say, therefore, that there is no God? Not at all! I can only
say that God isn't a blue crocodile. Science has done nothing but say that our definitions of God, so far, don't stand up
under investigation. But try this one on your reasoning pow-
ers: Science has proved that matter—*as* matter, at least—
doesn't exist: its reality exists only as energy. So materialists
are wrong when they try to see everything in material terms.
What they believe in is an unreality!"

"All right, but matter *is* real—in its own realm of vibration."

"So also are dreams. That is to say, if you hit your dream head against a dream wall, your dream head may hurt. And a few scientists have even suggested that life itself is really only a dream. A few others have declared that energy itself looks suspiciously like mere vibrations of thought."

"Yes, I've read that," said Isaac pensively. "But science says also that thoughts are only movements of energy in a circuit of nerve channels."

"Yet thoughts are vibrations of consciousness, which isn't produced by the brain. The scientist J. C. Bose, in India, demonstrated early in the twentieth century that even metals and rocks display a certain minimal degree of consciousness—enough to react to stimuli. The question is, Does the brain produce consciousness? Or is it merely the conduit for consciousness? Materialists tell us it produces consciousness. Yet matter doesn't exist—except, perhaps ultimately, as a vibration of consciousness. So then, how can the brain *produce* consciousness?"

"This discussion is getting fascinating. We've finished our coffee, but I can't think deeply while driving. So lets have lunch here? I'll be glad to pay for it."

"Thank you. And I'll be glad to accept!"

So we had lunch and continued our discussion. Over the salad, Isaac took a deep breath, then offered an objection: "Still, the facts you've mustered are a long way from indicating that there is a God."

"If we think of God as infinite consciousness, instead of as that blue crocodile I spoke about, and instead of as that bearded fellow on the ceiling of the Sistine Chapel in the

Vatican, we have something science hasn't disproved at all, and will never be able to disprove."

"Still, it all comes down to belief, and what science gives us are facts, not untested beliefs."

"But what if I tell you that there are people who *have* tested their beliefs, and have found them valid by their own actual, direct experience?"

"I'd say that personal experience is subjective, not objective, and therefore not universally true."

"And what would you say if countless thousands have had the same experience? that not one of those persons has ever contradicted another? that all of them have declared that finding God is the only true goal of life?"

"I'd say that it still isn't the same thing as producing something in a test tube for everyone to see, or as seeing it through the lens of a telescope, which enables all people to view the same thing."

"Right, not everyone can see God until his own consciousness is sufficiently refined. But everyone can make *himself* that test tube, that telescope. Only yesterday I was reminding someone that Jesus Christ said, 'Blessed are the pure in heart, for they shall see God.' Those who are pure in heart *do* see God. Thousands of men and women through the centuries, and in all countries, have claimed to see Him. The experiences they describe are all very similar."

"Hmm. Very well, then, I can visualize consciousness as the ultimate reality. Still, can you personalize an ocean of infinite awareness to the extent of believing that it may have, or can have, the slightest interest in our tiny human lives? To pray to such an ocean seems ridiculous! We might as well not even ponder the point. I mean, if all the stars and galaxies and nebulae—countless billions of them—are products of that postulated consciousness, how can it concern itself with tiny beings like you and me?"

"In fact, however, in the scale of objective size man's body is about halfway between the smallest and the largest body in existence. We aren't so tiny, after all!"

"Really? I didn't know that."

"Moreover, do we know where the center of the universe lies? I read a book of science once which stated that the electron holds the key to the whole universe. Could there be a center to this vast ocean of electrons?"

"Well, electrons are the building blocks of creation. Everything is made of electrons whirling through space. So then, even if there is consciousness behind it all, we are all just little whirling eddies of electrons!"

"Let's say that electrons, whirling eddies or not, are the building blocks. Yet if I left a load of building blocks in a jumbled pile out on an open field, they couldn't form themselves into a building. It takes an architect, and a builder, to construct a building. Moreover, just as a body must have a heart, and as a building of masonry must have a cornerstone, so there must be a center to it all. Where is the center of the universe—the cornerstone?"

"That's an absurd question!" he exclaimed. "For one thing, the universe isn't a work of masonry."

"No, but it needs a center. Every living thing grows from a seed. Even so, the universe must have grown outward from a central point. That's why science has evolved the Big Bang theory of Creation."

"I don't see that that follows at all. Can't the universe just come into existence—oh, all right, into *conscious* existence, spontaneously everywhere?"

"It could, if we postulated its center as being everywhere, and its circumference, nowhere."

"Okay, so where does that get us?"

"It gets us to this point: If we really want to understand the universe, or life, or even existence, we must approach it from within, at its own center in ourselves. But science doesn't do that. It might do so, if it turned its efforts inward, but it is preoccupied with skating over the surface of things. Isaac Newton, whose namesake you say you are, explained everything in terms of mass, weight, and motion. Well, he was in fact a very spiritual man, but in order to reach the materialistic consciousness of his age he had to measure, weigh, and time everything. His method will give you the shape of a planet, but it won't account for the particular vibrations that determine what we might call its astrological influence."

"Astrological! There you go, hauling in something out of the blue that is completely foreign to our discussion!"

"Well," I smiled, "I admit I said that to shock you! Though I think I might make a point for the inclusion of astrology. But the thing is, science can give you the outer facts of a case, but they can't give you its heart. It can give you how people behave, but it can't give you the motivations that make them behave as they do. And as to what those motivations might be, science can only guess at them."

"Are you saying that we can *know* levels of reality, from within, that have no outward correlation with one another?"

"Why not, if consciousness itself is the bridge? Think of it this way: If you tried to break through a field of ice by applying pressure over the whole field, the task would be virtually impossible. But if you drilled at one point, you'd find it relatively easy to penetrate through to the water underneath. Man will never be able to penetrate the mysteries of matter to the final reality beneath it, so long as he tries to do so outwardly. But if he goes within himself to his own center, he will find that he can break through that 'ice' with relative ease."

"And if he succeeds in reaching the water of truth underneath, will he lose himself?"

"That's what I still have to find out. I'm trying to lose myself."

"Well, I'm not! I don't like your way of thinking at all. Why should I forget myself?" He took a deep breath, then looked about as if for reassurance. "So then," he resumed, "according to you, I forget all about Isaac (me) and enter some sort of amorphous pool or ocean, lacking in all self-definition. What's in it for me? Why *should* I seek this God of yours? It seems to me you're on a mad quest. Why should I seek him, or it, or whatever you want to call it? What can you suggest that would make me even interested in doing so?"

I mused a moment, and then I said, "Why don't you try thinking of God as the highest aspect that you can imagine of your own self?"

"You mean, someone who is kind, and wise, and all forgiving? Well, yes, I can see something attractive in that. I mean, it would mean much less tension into my life. Yeah, I could live with that! But that would still be me. It wouldn't be God."

"Do you like music?" I asked with seeming irrelevance.

"Yes, sometimes," he answered, again with a hint of, "Where's all this heading?"

"If there's a piece of music that you particularly like, can you imagine its composer being dull or stupid?"

"Well, of course not!"

"Then if you think of God as the highest state of consciousness to which you can aspire—or shall we say, *beyond and above* that state of consciousness—can't you suppose that He must be even more enjoyable than that state?"

"Well, yes, though I must say you're drifting here into a sort of Sargasso Sea of speculation."

"Not really. Let me put it this way: What do all people really want in life?"

"A million things! Money, sex, pleasure, excitement, a new house, children: It would be beyond anyone's power to name them all."

"Yes, but in more general terms wouldn't you say that everyone in the world wants only two things: to avoid pain, and to find happiness?"

"Yes," said Isaac after a few moments of reflection. "Yes, I think that's true."

"The worst criminal, even if he defines happiness in terms of money, or power, or revenge, must really want these things—for no other reason than that he hopes to find happiness through them. Don't you agree?"

"Well, I guess that's obvious enough."

"The trouble is, he'll never find in those things what he really wants. Selfishness narrows his vision; happiness therefore eludes him. I'd go farther and say that he must therefore reincarnate again and again, until he finds the secret of true happiness. But for now let's ponder only the fact that everyone in the world is seeking only those two things: to avoid pain, and to find happiness. Why is this so?"

"Well, I don't know. Maybe it's just because pain hurts, and happiness makes you feel good."

"But if it were your actual nature to enjoy suffering, and if happiness only gave you another kind of pain—perhaps making you vomit—wouldn't you feel different? I'd put it rather this way: People enjoy happiness *because it is their own nature, as much as possible, to be happy.* And where did that nature come from?"

"From our DNA?"

I laughed. "Not if we are God's dreams. If dreams is all we are, it would have to mean that He Himself *is* that happiness. Indeed, He is much more than happiness. His nature is absolute Bliss. What we are seeking, in seeking Him (as all men do, whether consciously or not), is our own true Self—*as* bliss."

"Then are you saying that those who find Him, find bliss?"

"Yes. And from what I've read, the Bliss they experience is not only ever conscious and ever existing, but also ever *new*!"

"So the highest aspect of myself you were referring is, finally, perfect bliss? Well, that doesn't sound so bad!"

"The trouble is, what I've been telling you about has been only reasonable, and reason alone will never give you that experience. That's why I've said that feeling, apart from being the one thing man and science cannot create, is the most important reality of our existence. Reason is secondary. And the highest feeling, apart from bliss, is love. I would describe love as bliss in action."

"Bliss in action? I *like* that definition!"

"Moreover, when the action involves motion toward divine awareness, the most important feeling to have is the *desire* for that awareness. That is what is meant by devotion. Without devotion, we cannot approach God. There is no room here for cold, scientific logic. You can't analyze yourself to enlightenment. Even if what you want is wisdom, you must learn to *want* it—to love it. Indeed, the truest wisdom, ultimately, is love. To love perfectly is to know the secret of the universe."

"Well, I can see myself *desiring* bliss, but I can't see myself loving or being devoted to it. How can one love an abstraction?"

"That is where concessions need to be made to our humanity. After all, we, as human beings, are more naturally attracted to human forms than to abstract ideals. And it isn't *wrong* to think of God in human terms. After all, our separate existences are only His dream. As long as we know that it is the Infinite Consciousness which gazes at us from whatever form we worship, it is neither idolatry nor ignorance on our part to think of Him with form. To get to the roof of a building, we may need a ladder. You might say that God *with* form is our ladder. We may dispense with the ladder, once we've reached the roof. Once one reaches God, he no longer needs to think in such human terms. Yet from what I've read, many saints like to return from time to time to the sweetness of an I-and-Thou relationship with God."

"This is very interesting!" exclaimed Isaac. "I've taken

pride all my life in being objective and free from all emotional prejudice, but I see now that one's feelings can be
much deeper than mere emotions."

"Yes, emotions are reactive. We like this, or dislike that.
We may be angered by this, or pacified by that. We may
resent this treatment, or be gratified by that. But these
reactions relate back, always, to our own egos. We must
give up everything that swirls us back into the vortex of
ego-consciousness."

"And I suppose that means we should be humble. But
where's the joy in considering myself insignificant? If I see
myself as never having amounted to anything—as having
always been a sort of grey nonentity—I can imagine nothing
blissful or uplifting in that concept. To me, humility means
to reduce oneself to the level of your earthworm, creeping
slowly and helplessly on the ground, an open invitation to
get stepped on!"

"I'm afraid you've got a wrong slant on humility altogether.
You are tricking yourself back into ego-consciousness! That
kind of humility—self-abasement and self-deprecation—
is only another kind of self-definition: from saying, 'I am
everything!' to saying, 'I am nothing!' The truth is, in your
higher reality you really *are* everything! It's your ego that is
the delusion. Otherwise, there's joy in releasing one's hold
on egotism! When we can declare with conviction, 'Nothing
that I've done is mine. Nothing that I am is mine! Nothing
that I own is mine! Even I, myself, am not apart or separate
from anything else!' there comes a sense of blissful freedom
that is very far from any sense of loss or suppression. We

know, then, that there is a Higher Reality, and that in that
Reality we have our entire being."

"And that is what you call God?"

"That," I replied simply, "is what I call God."

"Then why—to come back to our earlier point—limit
God to a human form, if you want to rise above all forms?"

"That, again, is where the ladder comes in. To get out
of our own egos, we may think of them also in relation to
a higher reality: a child, for example, needing and *wanting* instruction from its parent. It's a mental image only, of
course, but it's an image that helps to lift our minds upward.
When battling ego-consciousness, we must use every trick
we can to get out of ego."

"Trick! That's a funny word," said Isaac, chuckling.

"Well, and why not? Isn't that what our egos do, also? We
earn money, and our ego tricks us into thinking the money
is really our own. We buy a house, and our ego tricks us into
thinking, 'This is mine!' Yet others owned that house before
us, and others will own it after us: Whose has it ever been,
really? We do something for which people praise us, but are
we in any way better for their praise? We do something else
for which they blame us—but are we, in ourselves, really
any the worse for their blame? We are what we are, no more
and no less, but our egos trick us into thinking that others can inflate or deflate us, like balloons! We may lose all
our money, but we will still be ourselves. Ego tells us that
we are diminished by outward losses, but in fact we remain
always the same. In success or in failure, in good health or
in disease, in popularity or in public excoriation, in wealth

or in abject poverty: we, in our true selves, remain forever unchanged. It is the tricks of ego that make us see ourselves each time differently. So, then, to think of ourselves as children of God is one way of offering ourselves up to that higher reality."

"Then that image in the Sistine Chapel isn't altogether wrong?"

"No, not altogether. Well, in fact there are two images of God in that chapel. One of them is behind the altar, showing a vengeful God whose energy is wholly directed in judgment against the poor damned. There's another one on the ceiling, where God is creating Adam. (Incidentally, if you look at Adam's raised knee and calf, you'll see there a suggestion of Eve's body, with breasts, soon to appear.) But if you want to think of God as something you can approach and love, why think of Him as judgmental? Why think of Him as ordaining your existence? In fact, why think of Him as a man at all? Couldn't 'He' just as easily be a 'She'? God made both men and women: 'He' is beyond all sexual distinction. The only reason we think of him as 'He' is that the masculine pronoun serves equally, at least in English, for mankind in general. It saves us from having to say 'It.' But even when I speak of God as 'He,' I personally think, 'She.' I like to think of God as my Divine Mother."

"Why?"

"Well, for one thing our mothers are often closer to us that our fathers. They are quicker to forgive us when we make mistakes. And they never stop loving us, even when we err seriously. When we are physically or emotionally hurt, we turn naturally to our mothers for comfort and healing. Most of all, I think, an instinct within us makes us look to our mothers as the source of our existence. And the beautiful thing is, when we think of the Divine Mother as that source, we can look to Her for inspiration in everything that we do. By living more in remembrance of that Source, we find a continuous flow of inspiration for further creativity. If we are painting, our works become more artistically beautiful. If we are sculptors, our works become more gracefully meaningful. If we are writers, whatever we write takes on new dimensions of truth. If we are in business, we find ourselves somehow making the right decisions in everything. And if we are cooks, our vibrations of love permeate the very food we cook, making it more delicious. It is easy to taste the difference between living food, cooked by our mothers who love us, and dead food that is cooked only mechanically—or even worse, food that is cooked without feeling, or with negative feelings like anger."

"But doesn't it feed the ego to do anything exceptionally well?"

"Not if you understand that it is really God—the Divine Mother—doing everything through you."

"Then how can I reduce my own self-definitions? By telling God, 'You did it'? Is that what you'll say? Okay, but I'm reminded here of the story of an Irish farmer who was visited by his local priest. The priest said to him, 'Sure and it's a fine family, O'Reilly, that you and God have created here. And it's a beautiful home that you and God have built.' Well, all of this the farmer accepted calmly enough. But when the priest went on to exclaim, 'And what a beautiful farm you and God have made here!' the farmer had to protest. 'Well,

Father,' he said, 'you may be right. But you should have seen this place when God had it all to Himself!' You can't be saying we must just passively let God do everything."

"No, we have to offer ourselves to him as co-creators, with Him. He has given us a beautiful world. We should try to make it an even better world. As God said, 'Be fruitful and multiply.' With the world population as high as it is, I'm not so sure He wants us to populate it further. But I do think He wants us all to try to leave it a little better than we found it. People today seem determined, unfortunately, to make it far worse! That's because they keep muddying the pond with that stick of their own egos! God never works directly in this world—except rarely, with miracles, and I'm not sure that even they don't require some sort of agency, even if the agent be only an angel. Otherwise, even as bees are needed to pollinate the flowers, so man is needed to work *with* God to improve this world and make it a place of ever-greater beauty. But when man goes against God, even the elements become disturbed. The important thing to realize is that we live in a *conscious* universe."

"So then, the natural disturbances with which we are all familiar, and which cause so much suffering—volcanoes, earthquakes, floods—are not only Nature's doing, but mankind's also?"

"Yes."

"Do you really believe that? And death, when it comes— are we responsible for that, also?"

"Death comes when our own actions of the past return to us, completing the cycle of action and reaction, of cause and effect."

"But could we prevent it?"

"Not even the longest-lived trees live forever. Death is necessary for the perpetuation of life. Constant renewal is needed to keep life ever fresh and interesting."

"Do you believe we have lived before? I know there are many people who claim so. And you hinted earlier that you do believe in reincarnation."

"If our consciousness were only something produced by the brain, reincarnation would be impossible. But if we owe our very ability to think to the simple fact that we are conscious already; if our brains are only transmitting stations, and not powerhouses that produce their own awareness; if life is not just an accident, and evolution not just happenstance but part of a deliberate, cosmic plan: then there must be a continuity somewhere."

"Well, all right then, how do you account for the mistakes: the simple fact that, if there were a cosmic plan, as you put it, there is imperfection everywhere? I mean, if you believe in God, isn't it impious to impute such fumbling to the Creator? Look not only at human babies born imperfect, but even animals—calves, let's say, born with five legs. Explain that to me!"

"I'd say your concept of perfection was very limited. It would leave no room for the turmoil necessary to keep Creation going and forever interesting. I spoke of God, and of Creation as well, as 'ever new.' That means that the show must have interest: suspense, surprise, the unexpected, even shock. Maybe that calf is a fallen human being who sinned in some way, and now needs to learn an important lesson. Maybe he was someone who interfered with everyone's life around him: a busybody who, in his busyness, seemed to be all arms! I'm being fanciful, but we're dealing here with fancies anyway. Certainly reincarnation explains human babies that are born with physical or mental defects."

"My God, you're turning my whole world topsy-turvy! But what about DNA, and genetics, and inherited traits? What about defects caused by mistakes of the mother while the baby is still in the womb?"

"Certainly a pregnant mother owes it to her baby to live rightly: to eat and drink correctly; to hold positive thoughts; to try to send divine blessings to the as-yet-unborn child. But even if she does all this, whatever happens will still be both the child's karma and her own. A child is not only the passive product of its parents: In descending from the astral world, when it is ready to be reborn, it goes to parents that are of a nature sympathetic to its own. Its mental traits are not inherited: they are brought over from before."

"Then what about physical traits that *are* inherited—obviously so—such as skin coloring?"

"Even that is a matter of attraction. The law of magnetism works much more subtly than people imagine. We are drawn to one another by the power of magnetic attraction."

"Now wait a minute! Just a minute. There you go, introducing another subject, and I don't know whether I can accept it. We all know that metals can attract one another, but what's all this about people attracting each other?"

"You must know, surely," I said, "that electricity passing through a wire produces also a subtle kind of magnetism? Energy generates a magnetic field. And all of us emit many kinds of energies. Electricity is only a gross kind of energy.

But love, too, is magnetic. So also are thoughts. You can attract greater success by expecting to be successful than by expecting to fail. And there are certain persons to whom you feel magnetically drawn, you just don't know why. There are others, too, for whom you may feel an instinctive aversion. The whole universe is, as I said, center everywhere. That means we ourselves, each one of us, are in the truest possible sense at its center! Our magnetism determines our own destiny. Everything that is drawn to us on our journey through life comes through this subtle law of magnetism: we *attract* it to ourselves. That's what they call in India the law of karma. There is no judge up in a cloud condemning us. We draw painful experiences to ourselves by our own wrong thoughts and actions in the past."

"But why should God make us suffer—or, if you prefer, why does He permit us to suffer—for our past mistakes? It seems almost vengeful on his part! We did them, but maybe now we've learned our lesson, and won't commit them again."

"Even so, deep in the subconscious mind there lingers a memory of having, let us say, cheated somebody. God is beyond all action, but that act on our part created a cause: we must allow the cause to complete itself in an effect. The cheating may have affected only one other person, but the very act of cheating put us, ourselves, to that extent out of harmony with the universal equilibrium. It created a wave, which must of its very nature be neutralized. For every upward wave there must be a corresponding trough. The underlying nature of reality is motionlessness. High waves cannot change the over-all ocean level. Every up is—and must forever be—balanced by a down; every emotional

high, by an emotional depression; every success, by a failure; every strike against others, by a strike against ourselves.
It all balances itself out in time. As to reincarnation, there
is an absolute need to be born again and again in order to
reach perfect equilibrium in ourselves."

"But I still don't see why a person—you say he retains
consciousness after death—can't just say, 'All right, I have a
new home now. I just don't want to go back to that old place.'
Why does he *have* to be reborn? I'm assuming you believe in
heaven. Well, if heaven is as beautiful as they claim it to be
(and I confess I've always laughed at the concept), why not
just stay there?"

"Well, the thing is, we live in a world of energy, not of
solid matter. If we want anything material, that magnetic
desire goes out from our heart-center toward that particular
object. We are magnetically drawn to it. And it, in turn,
is magnetically drawn to us. If we die with a longing for
cigarettes, for instance, we'll not be completely satisfied
even in heaven, for in heaven there is no air as we know it.
Something inside us will feel a lack. But I should add that a
desire for smoking is the smallest part of what draws souls
back from those realms. Every single desire in the heart, as
long as it is for anything material, must be satisfied here on
the material plane. Only refined desires—for example, for
uplifting music, or for beautiful scenery—can be satisfied
in the other world better than it can be here on earth. You
go to where your own desires, not necessarily your conscious
will, take you. A black person in this life may have been a
white person before who died bearing a prejudice against

blacks; he has been born black not only because his parents are black, but because his prejudice against that color created in him a magnetic aversion in that direction. And aversion, too, is magnetic. If you have tried all your life to help others, you will attract a better, or at least a good, rebirth in future lives because your own magnetism—which is a reflection of your karma—attracts you to them."

"Is it really possible for a human being to be reborn in an animal body?"

"I think it is. If, for example, one has spent his lifetime in finance, gobbling up other people's money and ruining their lives, he may have acted sufficiently like a tiger to be reborn as one! But I think human beings have reached a level of evolution where such a slip backwards must be rare, and surely only temporary."

"Is evolution itself not, as Darwin claimed, a matter of accident?"

"Darwin didn't take into account that there is consciousness everywhere. The consciousness even in a worm is impelled to rise toward its Source in Infinity. It is the impulse of all life to want to reclaim its own true reality. A leopard born without spots will, Darwin says, be at an evolutional disadvantage in the jungle, but the leopard is an intelligent animal. A sand-colored mutant will naturally seek an environment—perhaps a sandy desert—where it can move about unobserved."

"Then what about evil? If, as Einstein discovered, everything is relative, then can any act, really, be evil? A tiger must kill to live; so then is killing, in itself, bad? God, after

all, made the tiger! Good and evil must, then, be only relative. Modern thought insists that morality is only a matter of
social and family conditioning."

"Still, we don't live in a vacuum. Our actions, and the
quality of them, must relate to *something*. Einstein related
all movement to a constant: the speed of light. Morality,
similarly, must be related to something. I'd say that that
'something' was the divine bliss we are all seeking in our
own being. Whatever brings us closer to perfect bliss in ourselves is good for each of us. And whatever obscures that
bliss is evil. Murder is wrong primarily because it denies
another person the right to live and, to that extent, suf-
focates that sense of right in our own selves. Human law
punishes people for murder, and rightly so; after all, society
must be protected against unnecessary turmoil. But people's
own nature punishes them even more severely. Even if a
person is not conscious of having a conscience, the life force
within him shrinks at the thought of having denied that life
in another human being. We must always try to be harm-
less—to radiate blessings outward to the world around us."

"Gosh! What a world you're opening up for me! Life, as
you see it, is not only true, but beautiful! I've spent my own
life like a dry leaf: analyzing, doubting, questioning. Now
I think the only thing in life is to change my course altogether, and to look for what will give me joy! I like your idea
of a loving God—a Cosmic Mother. Thank you, Friend." He
held out his hand to me, not knowing what else to do. But
I could see in his eyes a gratitude that welled up from his
heart. I answered him:

"It hasn't been all one way, you know. I, too, have gained

greatly from this encounter. You've helped me to understand many things. For, in articulating my ideas, they've become clearer in my own mind. I'm on a quest for understanding. The greatest thing I've come to understand through our conversation is that, apart from ridding myself of all self-definitions, I must love my Divine Mother ever more intensely. It's Her I'm seeking. My quest is for Her. And I'm finding Her everywhere—in you, in the sheer beauty of truth, even in this food we've been eating. I will never forget you."

We went out arm in arm to his car. He continued some ten miles down the road. Then we came to a branch off it.

"Unfortunately, I must turn off here," he said. "Goodbye, Friend. Thank you for everything. I hope your quest is fully successful."

We parted with expressions of good will. As his car vanished, I looked up into the clouds overhead. And there, unexpectedly, I saw Our Lady of Guadalupe smiling down at me and gently nodding Her head, as if to say, "Very good!"

SIX

A Materialist

I HAD GONE PERHAPS TWO MILES DOWN THE ROAD when a large car stopped by me, a Cadillac, and chauffeur driven. The rear window nearest me rolled down, and a voice barked:

"Get in!" It was virtually a command.

"Thank you," I replied courteously. "I don't mind if I do."

Stepping in, I beheld beside me a large, imposing man. He spoke loudly, with an air of brusque efficiency.

"Name's Bolton. Are you on the tramp?" he demanded.

"I'm not quite sure what you mean," I said.

"Have you no job?"

"I'm without a job, without a home, without a country, without a name, without any particular reality at all."

"What kind of answer is that?"

"I'm on a quest for understanding. I guess you could say, on a quest for *self*-understanding."

"Sounds goofy to me! I saw you in that restaurant back there. I couldn't hear the discussion you were having with your friend, but you looked like a competent citizen. I thought there might be something in you. Yet here I find you walking alone. Do you need a job? I might be able to offer you one."

"Thank you, but I don't want a job. Please tell me," I said, "what do you consider the purpose of life?"

"What kind of question is that?"

"You've asked me if I need a job. Is that your purpose in life—to earn money?"

"Well, what else is there? Of course it's to earn money—to become rich. I guess I've been luckier than most. I have ten thousand people working for me, a twenty-room mansion, and a yacht: a handsome sailboat. I have everything I want. And you could have what you want—or, anyway, much more than you seem to have right now."

"What if I don't want anything?"

"That isn't possible! A man needs money. He needs possessions. He needs a home, security. Things like that are basics."

"Have you read what Jesus said about not building on sand?"

"What are you talking about?"

"He was speaking of the foolishness of building one's home on shifting foundations. You've described money and possessions as fundamental needs. I'm saying that anyone who bases his happiness on them is likely to find it tumbling down around him some day. He'll be lucky to come out alive!"

"Nonsense! I have insurance. My home and everything in it is insured. Nothing can go wrong."

"What about your body?"

"I have health insurance."

"Are you insured against disease? Are you insured against getting cancer, or some other fatal illness?"

"Of course not."

"Have you a wife?"

"Yes."

"Are you insured against her dying?"

"Obviously, my insurance can't cover that. Nor can I insure against the death of my children. It would be stupid to expect that."

"And if your mansion burns down, I suppose you'll be reimbursed?"

"Of course."

"But can your insurance bring back all the objects you've so lovingly gathered in your home?"

"No, that would be a loss, I admit. Still, with money I could replace the loss with other objects. I can't insure my life, but I can insure that the family I leave behind me is well off."

"What about a stock market crash? Businesses do go bankrupt. What about your business? There's no absolute certainty of its continued success. What if public interest in what you have to sell disappears? What if a rival appears and tries to steal your business?"

"Ha! I'll demolish him!"

"Do you like demolishing people?" I asked.

"It's the salt of life!" he replied with an aggressive grin. "Beat or get beaten. Kill or get killed. That's the way to keep one's heart pumping."

"Until it stops," I remarked. "Tell me: Are you relaxed with this attitude toward life?"

"No. But who needs relaxation?"

"Are you happy?"

"Not yet, maybe. But I surely will be."

"What will make you happy?"

"Having more of everything."

"But don't you see that, as long as you're seeking more, you'll never have enough?"

That stopped him! He gave me a look of surprise.

"What're you getting at?"

"I'm saying that desire has a momentum of its own. You expect to arrive finally at the train station, but if momentum itself is your entire reality, you'll never reach a station. I'm saying that, without inner peace, happiness will forever elude you."

"But—a person has to earn money in life."

"There is certainly a need to meet life's basic necessities, but what is the point of accumulating more and more money? What can you do with it?"

"Well, one never knows what else he might want. I have a mansion, a yacht, but I might get many other things, over time: a helicopter; more land, a mountain villa in Aspen, Colorado—the possibilities are endless."

"Yes, and all that would feed your sense of importance, right?"

"Well, of course. I *am* important in this world. People look up to me. The more they envy me, the more important I feel."

"The bigger the balloon, however, the louder the pop when it bursts."

"Well, I'd like to see anyone try to pop *my* balloon! I'd smash him."

"So, with this attitude, you're always prepared to do battle."

"*Semper* something or other: Be prepared. Isn't that the boy scout motto?"

"But to be prepared for *battle?* That means to be tense. It means to feel fear. Even if you're sure of winning, you will be tense, and with your tension, you won't be able to help being uncertain. With uncertainty moreover, as I said, there will be fear. No, your whole attitude speaks of tension, fear, peacelessness, and unhappiness. Without peace, happiness is simply impossible."

My companion reflected a long moment. Finally his voice became softer, less aggressive.

"Well," he continued, "I must admit I don't really have peace of mind. And you've put your finger on something else: I'm not really happy; I only hope to *become* happy someday. And you're right: I *am* tense all the time. I don't know why I'm telling you these things. Maybe it's just because I don't know you. I sure wouldn't tell anyone else! But I guess behind my drive for success there *is* fear. Still, I do want to keep on earning money. It's a momentum I've built up. I don't even *want* to stop!"

"I see your problem. And, considering that momentum, I doubt you could stop it now even if you wanted to. But do you think you might be able to deflect it?"

"How do you mean?"

"Well, consider: The reason money itself is attractive is not money itself. It's all those glitzy things money can buy! One desire fulfilled only leads to other desires for fulfillment. A million desires, fulfilled, can never ensure satisfaction! Millions more desires will simply leap into the breach. It's a never-ending treadmill, with promises of fulfillment shining into the sky just beyond the horizon, or singing to you from just around the next corner. And meanwhile, the more money you have, the more numerous the fulfillments you imagine, until life itself could never bring you the time to fulfill even a tithe of them. Wealth is a delusion!"

"My God! I guess it's because I don't know you, but between the two of us I'll confess I've often wondered if I wasn't on a treadmill. It's work, work, work—day in, day out. Even when I'm on vacation, I'm phoning the office to make sure everything is going smoothly, or phoning my stock broker to see if I can seize the opportunity to invest in something hot before it's too late."

"And so life will slide by, and what will you have accomplished? I'm reminded of an American Indian who had a small quarter-acre piece of land, and a small house. A land-wealthy neighbor befriended him. One day this neighbor said to him, 'It pains me to see you working that tiny plot of land, and living in relative poverty. Let me give you five acres. I can easily spare them, and it will help you to be more affluent.' The Indian said, 'I thank you sincerely for this offer. But really, I can't accept it. You see, if I had to work more land, I wouldn't have the time for singing.' Don't *you* want time, also, for singing? Peace of mind is the most priceless treasure of all. Without it, man cannot enjoy anything!"

"Peace! Say, the more you talk about it, the more I find it appealing. What can I do? I'm saddled on a runaway horse. If I tried to get off at this speed, I'd probably be killed. What hope is there for me?"

"I can make one important suggestion to you. You've been thinking in terms of accumulating. What about thinking, now, in terms of sharing your gains with others? Don't worry," I hastened to add, "I want nothing from you! But there is great need in the world, and there *is*, as you pointed out, a need for money everywhere. If you use your money to gratify other people's *needs*—not their desires—you will find, in the giving, that your inner tension will decrease; you'll have greater peace of mind, and with that, more happiness."

"But what happiness can there be in giving anything of mine to someone else? He isn't me. His sorrows are his own, and so are his joys. It seems to me I should be concerned with my own happiness."

"Certain realities of life," I said, "need thinking over. Have you noticed, let's say, a little child when it falls and gets bruised? It may cry loudly. But if it's playing a game and falls, he may not even notice the fall: he just gets up and keeps on playing. Why? His second fall may give him an even worse bruise, but the difference is, he isn't thinking of himself: he's thinking about the game. Self-involvement is the source of all our suffering—not some of our suffering only: all of it! The more a person thinks of himself, the more he's affected by everything. His fears are exaggerated. He feels pain more intensely. He not only regrets loss: he *suffers* over even the slightest loss, over every little setback.

On the other hand, when you are at the movies and you see the hero winning a great victory, let us say, don't you feel like cheering?"

"Yes, it's true, I do! And when he loses something important to him, maybe his mother—I remember, one time, I wept!"

"That's because you identify with those people on the screen. And why should you do so? They aren't you. Or are they? What makes you separate from them? The cells of your body change constantly. It is said that our bodies change completely every seven years. We might say they are nothing but holding patterns for a succession of material that just passes through them. You aren't really that body: you're only a 'holding pattern.' So then, what about the life that animates your body? Is it really your own? You are connected to others around you if only in this way: if everyone around you is miserable, it is next to impossible for you to be happy. And if everyone around you is happy, you, too, are much more likely to be happy. In other words, their consciousness affects you. The reverse is true also: if you are happy in yourself, your happiness is contagious. It affects others."

"Well, that much is obvious. Certainly, others affect us to that extent, and we also affect them."

"Moreover, the more you consciously *emanate* happiness, instead of keeping it to yourself, the more others will feel that happiness also."

"That much too, I think, is obvious."

"Again, the more you make others happy, the happier you are, too."

"Yes. I can see that."

"When you live for yourself alone, and don't share yourself with others, not only do they get no happiness from you: you, too, become unhappy."

"Are you speaking personally?"

"No, what I'm saying is true for everybody. The more we give of ourselves, the more we find happiness. And the more we try to absorb for ourselves, the less happiness we find. We can possess everything we ever dreamed of, and still be miserable—or at least deeply dissatisfied, and unfulfilled. In giving of ourselves, we find satisfaction; in taking, we find dissatisfaction. And why? because giving is expansive; taking, or absorbing into oneself, is contractive. The more you live in your ego, the less happy you will be. Ego only masquerades as our entire reality, and is really the cause of all our suffering. Thinking of others, and being concerned for their wellbeing, is the beginning of true happiness."

"Still, I have to say I've found great pleasure in collecting things."

"Have you ever tried giving things away?"

"I can't say that I ever have. Not things that I prize. Oh, I've given presents to people. I've given them things I thought they might like. But of the things I've liked for myself: no, I don't think I've ever given those away. To me, it would be a sign that I didn't truly value them."

"If you look at it another way, the value you place on them needn't be that of ownership, but of simple appreciation. To enjoy things impersonally is one thing, but to appoint yourself as their custodian, with all the care and responsibility they require, is quite another. As their custodian you must protect them from damage and from theft. Worse still, they add to your self-definitions. You think, 'This is *mine!*' They become chains, preventing you from free movement."

"And yet it's a pleasure to own them."

"A pleasure, yes. But pleasure is not happiness. Pleasure is really nothing but a nerve stimulant—like, one might say, a mosquito bite!"

"Well, I'd hardly compare the satisfaction of owning a fine work of art to a mosquito bite!"

"Why not? There's pleasure in scratching a mosquito bite, but there's also pain. And in ownership also there's both pleasure and pain. In some ways the pain of ownership is worse, because it binds you. I'd say that one can feel really free inside if he can find equal pleasure in giving away whatever he owns."

"I'm not sure I'm equal to that. I have a fine Picasso, for example which I look at daily. If I gave it away, I wouldn't be able to enjoy seeing it anymore."

"Picasso," I said musingly. "Do you really like looking at it? What sort of painting is it?"

"Well, it has a split face—I'd say sort of schizophrenic."

"And do you feel pleasure, looking at it?"

"Well, not pleasure exactly, at least not so much in the message. But I feel pride in looking at it and in knowing that I own it."

"The thought, 'It's valuable; it's mine; I beat out the competition in buying it!' Is that what you mean?"

"Well, yes, I guess so. Yes, I guess that *is* what I mean." He looked at me a little ruefully.

"I think of a good work of art as a friend: as someone I'd

like to invite into my home because I like him; because he makes me feel good."

"Yes, I do see what you mean. Owning that Picasso pleases my ego, rather than my actual sense of the fitness of things."

"I'm not suggesting you give your Picasso away. But we've spoken of the pleasure of ownership. Have you considered the still greater pleasure of *non*-ownership? The happiness that comes from giving, from sharing that pleasure of ownership with others, by giving them things that you prize? I've found greater happiness come from denying myself the pleasure of—well, I'll put it bluntly: of selfishness."

"My God!" expostulated Mr. Bolton. "You're taking me down a long, dusty road!"

"From competition to cooperation! From being surrounded by enemies to surrounding oneself with friends. Which, do you think, can bring you the greater happiness? With the one there's tension, and fear, and peacelessness. With the other, there's security, and peace of mind and heart. With the first, there's the hollow satisfaction—if you win!—of having beaten your enemies. With the second there's the knowledge that you're supported on all sides by the people you know. Which is better?"

Musingly he said, "And with the one, there's the thought, I'm using ten thousand people to increase my own wealth and power. But with the other there's the thought, I'm helping ten thousand people to live useful, rewarding lives. I find this thought much more satisfying. Thank you!"

"I want to thank you, too. In talking these things through, I've understood many things more clearly. As I said back when we met, I'm on a quest for understanding. I'm not 'on the tramp,' as you suggested. I'm not looking for a job. But I have a deep desire to find out what life is all about. And it helps me very much to clarify in my own mind what life is *not* all about. Life isn't something to be seized. It's given us to be offered! The more we offer it back in a spirit of expansion to its source, the more self-fulfilled we feel. All of us belong to a higher Reality. But I'm not asking you to follow me in that thought! It's enough for you to understand that you'll get more out of life if you share its pleasures with others than if you seize power, wealth, and possessions for yourself alone, or even if you seek importance in the eyes of others."

We came to a small town. As we reached the center of it, Mr. Bolton said, "Here's where we part ways. Mine lies in a different direction now. Please tell me, Friend: Is there anything I can do for you?"

"Really," I answered, "there's nothing I want. Thank you, though."

"But it wouldn't be right if I didn't in some way show my gratitude to you for the insights you've given me. Let me at least pay for your stay at this inn," he concluded, pulling up in front of a small building.

"I'd be grateful for that. I'll accept, for your sake. And I wish you much happiness in your life. I feel blessed to have met you."

"I really appreciate that. And I appreciate *you*. Thank you."

He left me with a warm glow in my heart. God and truth exist equally in all men. Everyone, really, is seeking only one thing: God's bliss. His conscious desire is to attain it at whatever level he is able in his present state to understand.

SEVEN

Sense Addicts

As I awoke the next morning, I was granted another vision of Our Lady of Guadalupe. I only saw Her; I couldn't touch Her. She appeared with Her arms slightly extended, palms upward, as though bestowing grace—though in fact She had a slightly teasing look, and She was lifting Her hands alternately as if to say, "Which will you choose?" A moment later She disappeared.

So what have we now? I asked myself. Some divine mischief afoot?

I left the inn shortly after breakfast, and set off down the road again, walking some miles. It was another day for singing, but this time I was more pensive. Our Lady intends something for me today! I thought, and wondered, Will it be an ordeal? I felt slightly uneasy.

After some time, a car stopped beside me. A young couple in the front seat smiled and said, "Would you like a ride?"

"Is this the ordeal?" I asked Our Lady with an inward smile. I then opened the back door.

At that moment, a young woman in back sat up. She'd

been reclining on the seat. Now she smiled at me provoca-tively. I was about to back away, when I remembered my vision.

"Is this what you have in mind, Mother?" I asked men-tally. "Is it something you want me to face in my quest for understanding?" I felt Her smile—teasingly—in my heart, but with a sense of reassurance.

Getting in, I addressed the couple in front. "Thank you."

"Are you going far?" the woman asked.

"As far as God cares to lead me," I replied. "I'm on a quest."

"A *quest*! So what are you seeking—a job? a lost relative? a new life?"

"I'm seeking for understanding," I replied.

"Understanding!" The woman turned around and stared at me. "What's there to understand?"

"Life," I said. "What it means. Why we are here in these bodies. Why we were born here on earth."

"Well," she said with a light laugh, "you could hardly have been born anywhere else!"

"But why was I born at all? I don't expect you to under-stand. I just felt I should answer you truthfully. The people I've been meeting on the road have helped me toward that goal. Maybe you will, too," I suggested with a smile.

She flounced back into her former position. "Well, I can't imagine how," she commented dismissively. "I mean, here we are, born, and trying to make the best of it."

"Yeah!" the man commented. "The meaning of life—well, that's simple enough! It's to live it up! have fun! enjoy!"

"And what do you enjoy?" I asked.

"Why, life! Going places. Doing things."

"Things," I repeated. "What things?"

"Dancing; parties; singing; music; good food; lots of drink. Fun. Excitement! Yeah, that says it all: We want excitement. That's what life's all about, until you're too old to enjoy anything—and then you might as well be dead!"

Reflecting on my church-going friends, I remarked with amusement, "Then I take it you don't go to church on Sundays?"

"Church? Hell, we're both too hung over Sunday mornings to go anywhere—except maybe to the local McDonald's for a cup of coffee."

"And that, to you, is living?"

"Well, listen to their hymns in church! The words alone would put you to sleep quicker'n any bottle of whiskey. I *know*. My mom used to take me there. And the *sermons*! My God, I passed my boyhood getting sermonized out of my wits. 'Do God's will'! I'd ask Mom, What about *my* will? What do I care what God wants? Let Him mind His own business, I say, and I'll mind mine."

"Well, you seem to have your philosophy of life pretty well worked out." I was prepared to dismiss him from my mind.

The young woman at my side gave me a seductive glance and remarked, "They say it takes two to tango. They," a nod of her head indicated the two in the front seat, "are a couple. What do you say we make a couple, too? You're nice looking. You're still young enough to have fun!"

"Divine Mother," I prayed silently, "is this Your teasing?" To the young woman I said, "So what does that make us? a couple of back seat drivers?"

"Oh, come on big boy. You're a man. I'm a woman. Doesn't

that mean something to you?" She thrust her breasts out provocatively and gave me a coy look.

"So what are you offering me? Flesh touching flesh. Flesh," I repeated disdainfully: "carrion, which someday will be rotting on a bare skeleton!" I tried not to show my disgust.

"My God! What're you saying?!"

"You don't know me. I don't know you. I don't even know your name."

"My name's Susan."

"All right, Susan," I answered severely. "I don't know that I'll even tell you my name. It doesn't matter. I know your name now, but I don't know *you*. You don't know me. For all you know, if we did know one another we wouldn't be compatible at all. We're *people*, not just bodies. We're human beings, with our own special traits, likes, ambitions, longings. I know nothing about yours; you know nothing about mine. What's this about being a couple? A couple of what: turtles?"

"Oh my God, what've I got sitting beside me?"

"A fellow turtle," I said. "Draw in those feelers of yours. Get back into your shell. That's all your skin is. By touching you, I'd only be touching a shell."

"Hey, just a minute! What're you talking about?"

From the front seat, the man spoke up. "Say, I've been listening to you two. There's something weird going on. Turtles, you say? I think I may have been wrong to pick you up."

"Don't you see?" I said. "You talk of pleasure; excitement. And then you talk of hangovers. Don't you realize that after *every* pleasure there's a kind of hangover? Every high is followed by a low. Every up of excitement is followed by a down of depression. You're bobbing through life like a yo-yo!"

"Hmm," he said. "That's a new thought! You know, I'd like to hear you out. There's something in what you say that rings a bell. I want to say, 'What's wrong with you?' But I think I'd better give you a chance to explain yourself. Let's stop at the next restaurant and have lunch together. I want to talk."

Susan, sitting beside me, sulked. Obviously she felt she'd been insulted. We traveled in silence the next mile or two. Finally we came to a restaurant, and stopped.

"Lets go in here," the man said. "We can talk over our meal."

The four of us went inside. Susan wouldn't even look my way. She held her arms close to her side.

We sat at a table for four. The couple sat facing each other; so did Susan and I.

"My name's Jake. This is my wife, Mary. And you've met Susan. What's your name?"

"Friend," I said.

"That's one I haven't heard before. German origin? Anyway, Mr. Friend, what you said back there intrigued me. It matches my experience. I'd like to hear more."

We placed our order for food. He then continued, "So now, you were right about the yo-yo. I do see that my life has been a succession of ups and downs, of highs and lows. Yes, pleasure and excitement have always ended in depression of some kind. But does it have to be so?"

"It does," I answered. "Life is like a swing. You can't keep moving on in one direction. Sooner or later, you'll have to swing back again. The farther forward you swing, moreover, the farther you'll swing back in the opposite direction. You'll never find permanent satisfaction if you keep swinging away from your own center."

"But swinging can be fun!" protested Mary. "The wider the arc, the better."

"No, but I know what he means," said Jake. "I've been feeling for some time now that things aren't clicking quite as they ought to. We go to a party, and the next morning, even if we didn't drink, I feel empty. That *is* a kind of hangover too, isn't it? We go dancing, laugh, enjoy the beat, and afterward when we're alone, isn't there a sort of let down? And even with you, Mary, I've noticed that when you carp at me the most is just after we've been the closest together."

Mary seemed a little irritated. "I don't know what you're talking about, Jake. One's moods change, naturally, but I don't see any pattern to them. That's just life. We can't always be the same; that would be boring!"

"No, but I've begun to notice a pattern. Excitement pumps me up, but then it drains me. I used to figure that was just how things were, but I've begun to wonder. And now," he turned to me, "you've suggested there's an alternative. I'd like to hear more about what that is."

"Think of it this way," I said. "There is the *power* to enjoy; and there are the things we enjoy. These two aren't the same at all. You think you are enjoying things, but in fact you're only *projecting* joy onto them! That is why two people may enjoy quite different things. The food that gives you pleasure may not even taste good to another person. The drink you like, another man may dislike. Your enjoyment, you see, comes not from things, but from yourself. The displeasure you feel comes from yourself. By trying to enjoy things, you give energy to them; you don't get energy from them. The more you give out in excited expectation to the world, the more drained of energy you become."

"So where does my energy come from?"

"It comes from inside yourself! You get it from the source of life, from the simple fact that you're alive. By continued expectations of receiving from life, however, you drain yourself of life. You'll grow old quickly. In some ways you're an old man already, Jake! You don't look at things with a fresh gaze anymore. You're getting jaded. Your enthusiasm is becoming more and more an affirmation. I've seen these symptoms many times before, again and again."

"My God! Why don't they teach us these things in school? This is much more important than physics, or than learning about evolution! They ought to teach us how to live."

Mary chimed in, "You say he doesn't look with a fresh gaze. I worry that his gaze is altogether too fresh sometimes, when looking at other women!"

I smiled. "Even so," I said, "it's energy he's giving out, not energy he's receiving."

"Look, let's not get into that subject!" Jake said. "The point—the real point—is, I really am losing the bright feeling I used to have. There's something wrong with the way I'm living, and that includes you, Mary. You know I'm right. They ought to teach us these things in school. Why do we have to learn them later on, maybe after it's too late? Yes, I'd like to change. But . . ."

"Yes," I said, "But—there's always the power of habit."

"There's habit," Jake repeated. "*Can* I change? I'm not sure *we* can. That thought scares me. It may be too late."

"You're still relatively young," I said. "After forty, it's much harder. But if, even now, you exert will power, you'll be able to redirect your energies. The first thing to do is, change the company you keep."

"I can't see doing that," said Mary. "Our friends are our *friends*: they're not just company. I'd hate to let them down." Mary, obviously, was less keen about the thought of change. I didn't want to impress her further with the need for it. Every human being has a right to grow in understanding at his own pace.

"But *self*-control is the main thing," said Jake.

"That's the first thing God asks of you," said I.

"God? It's always seemed to me that He wanted to control *me*!"

"That's what the churches teach, but it isn't what the Bible teaches. He gave every man free will. This is our most sacred right."

"So I'm right: in the end it's my will, not God's, that matters."

"Yes, and no. God wants only your happiness, but your will, if you lack wisdom, may lead you to *un*happiness. A man needs to be rightly guided, from within. God won't force Himself on anyone, but a man must learn where his own best interests lie. You'll please God best if you'll try following His ways."

At this point, Susan came out of her sulks to blurt out: "He, Him, man, men: I'm sick of hearing those words! Even God, they say, is a man. What about us women? Where do we fit in? Are we just the bones of Adam's rib? Women are as good as men—better in many ways, in fact. We do better in school. We'd do better in business, too, when men let us. We're suppressed, and why? Just because men have the muscles!"

I laughed—not at her, but with her. "You're perfectly right, Susan," I said. "Men have more muscles, but the main difference between men and women is that men go more by reason, and women, more by feeling. And when a woman's feelings are calm—as yours aren't just now, I should mention—women are often more insightful than men. Reason chops things into little pieces, making them into a disjointed jigsaw puzzle. Calm feeling, however, is soul-intuition, which sees things whole and not piecemeal."

"So you *do* give us credit for something!"

"Of course. It's when you think of yourself as a woman, not as a soul, that you, too, become fragmented. The reason men have always been at the forefront is that men's energy is more outward. But it's also because for centuries we've been living in a dark age of matter-consciousness. Matter, too, can be fragmented, as energy cannot be. The best way of dealing with matter is through reason. Lately, however, we entered a new age of energy. Today, we know that matter is only a vibration of energy. Because energy is flowing and not fixed, women in every field will be coming to the fore. I shouldn't be surprised if they didn't end up at the forefront in many fields. The one thing that might prevent that from happening is not intelligence, but inclination. Women's natural inclination, as I remarked, is inward rather than outward."

"Say," cried Mary, "I'm beginning to like you! What you're saying makes sense. I think one thing that irritates me about Jake—and mind you, I love him—is his attitude of knowing everything!"

"But here, today," said Jake, "I'm learning. And it's exciting."

"There you go," I said, "equating excitement with happiness! The two are quite different. The more you let yourself succumb to excitement, the *less* you'll ever know of happiness. In seeking self-control, you should control above all your desires and emotions."

"Gosh, that isn't what I've been taught at all! Even the music we listen to is intended to excite our emotions."

"Music's another thing," I said, "that has a very great influence on our consciousness. The heavy beat of modern music almost forces people to live in and through the body; to beat their feet in affirmation of earthliness; to shake and nod their heads in ego-affirmation. Did you know that the ego is centered in the medulla oblongata, at the base of the brain? When you toss your head about like a rock singer, you're really screaming, 'I—I—*I*!' As long as you affirm your ego like that, your will power will always be guided by the desire for excitement and stimulation. It can never be guided by wisdom."

"Gee, you never let up, do you? I can see that I've a long way to go before I find the happiness I'm really seeking, but at least I feel you've started me on a worthwhile journey. Thank you very much, Mr. Friend. I appreciate this meeting. And no, I don't think you're weird at all. You make sense."

"I appreciate meeting all of you, also," said I. "For I've

learned what a pitfall the senses can be. I'd rather forgotten that. It will pay me to be very careful from now on. As long as I'm on this pilgrimage, I'm likely to encounter traps for the unwary. Thank you for the warning."

"And I want to thank you, too," said Susan unexpectedly. "I see now that what I was doing earlier was motivated by a wish to take power from you: to become, in a sense, greater than you. But if we're equal, I don't need to do that! I can come on in a more giving way. I see now that male-female relationships can be more relaxed if they are based on mutual respect."

"I'm glad you understand, Susan. I felt nothing against you, personally. It was your attitude I was fending off."

I decided to leave them there. I wanted to be alone for awhile, to think things out a little. As I left the restaurant (yes, they paid for the meal!), I looked up into the clouds. Our Lady of Guadalupe was smiling, and there was no teasing in Her smile this time. I began to sing as I continued on my way.

EIGHT

The Monks and the Church

S ome distance down the road, I came upon a car standing by the wayside. Outside it were three monks wearing brown habits. One of them was replacing a flat tire; the other two were seated nearby on a grassy bank, watching the operation.

"Greetings, strangers," I said.

"Greetings, brother," they replied smiling.

"You look as though you didn't need help. But would you like more company?"

"Please join us," they said graciously, and I did so.

As I settled myself on the bank beside the two "non-combatants," I asked them humorously, "So, do you think God may have arranged for you to have this flat tire just so that we might meet?"

"Who knows?" they both answered. Then, with equal good humor, one of them continued, "His ways are inscrutable. He might have taken time out from overseeing the fate of nations, or the slow movement of galaxies, to give thought to so small a thing as this meeting."

"Do you suppose," I wondered aloud, "he even sees things in terms of big and small? Is He Himself big? Is size an attribute we can apply to Him? In other words, do you think He may be some sort of giant, overseeing the whole universe from outside it, or above it?"

At this, the brothers became more serious. "The universe," one of them said, "exists outside of Him. We don't know what He looks like, but we do know He made us all."

"And how do you imagine He made us?" I inquired. "Out of nothing?"

"It can only have been so, for we are taught that God is 'wholly other.' It would be presumptuous to think otherwise."

"You say, 'We are taught.' Are your personal beliefs the result only of someone else's teaching? or are they the result of your own reflection?"

"Well, of course we abide by the dogmas taught by our Church."

"Do you believe, then, that your church is always right?"

"Well," said one of them, "I don't think anyone would go that far. By the way, I am Brother Augustus. This," he indicated the monk seated closer to me, "is Brother Pacificus. And that," he indicated the monk changing the tire, "is Brother Francis." In time I discovered Brother Augustus to be rather austere by nature, and slightly aloof. Brother Pacificus was altogether different from what his name suggested: a little restless, and of a jovial nature. Brother Francis was simple, and displayed a devotional temperament.

Brother Augustus continued somewhat pontifically, "Protestants have gone to great lengths to point out the Church's mistakes. Among their criticisms are those of Mar-

tin Luther: the sale of indulgences. They point also to the
extreme lack of charity demonstrated by the Spanish Inqui-
sition. I think any reasonable man would agree at least with
those criticisms. Still, we believe that the Church, despite
its mistakes, represents most truly the teachings and legacy
of Jesus Christ.

"It is well," he added, "that one body, and even one person—the Pope—decide what Jesus meant, rather than
let people randomly make up their own minds as to what
he meant. In unity there lies strength: in division lies the
potential for dissolution."

Brother Pacificus smiled. "We've told you our names.
What's yours?"

"When we met, you addressed me as 'brother.' Let's just
stay with that name: not Brother something-or-other; just
Brother. I'm trying to forget my name. I want to obliterate
every sense of self-identity. I'm on a quest for understanding, and I know what I *don't* want to be. I'm trying to discover who and what I really am."

"Well," said Brother Francis, "I think we should honor
that. But surely you understand at least that you were created by God."

"That's part of my problem," I said. "What does it mean,
to be created by God? Did He make us, as a potter molds
clay? If so, where did He get the clay? I see another alternative: He must have *become* us."

"Why, He made us, surely," said Francis, "indeed as a potter molds clay. The Bible implies that we are fundamentally
different from Him. Only Jesus was His actual Son."

Augustus added, "St. Paul said that, if we believe in Jesus

Christ, we are God's children by adoption. Otherwise, there is no hope for us."

"But if He made us, out of what could He have made us?"

Brother Pacificus said with a laugh, "I don't see any problem there. He just made us. Isn't that enough?"

"To my mind, it isn't nearly enough! You're saying he produced everything as if out of thin air. But there can't even have been thin air, then. Nothing can come out of nothing! There must be at least something existing for the universe to appear."

"But Catholic dogma," said Augustus, "dating back two thousand long years, says that it did. Who are we to question it? Who are we to doubt what wiser heads than ours have declared?"

"What makes them wiser?" I asked. "Who declares their wisdom? Is their antiquity their only credential?"

"Tradition gives them weight," Augustus replied. "The fact that tradition endorses what they said is sufficient."

"Besides tradition," said Brother Francis, "when we pray to God, we pray to someone other than ourselves."

"Well, we may be praying to our *higher* Self. Basically, however, I don't think truth can be institutionalized, if only because institutions are biased. For one thing, the unwritten guideline of every institution is self-preservation. Yet the need for self-preservation makes self-interest a priority. Where self-interest is involved, truth takes a back seat."

"Are you a Christian?" asked Brother Pacificus with a smile.

"I like to think of myself as one," I replied.

"What church do you belong to?"

"I belong to no church. The life and teachings of Jesus Christ are one thing, but our experience of them depends on our own experience of life. People's experiences of life vary. There must be as many types of Christianity as there are Christians."

"You make a strong argument," said Brother Francis, straightening up. He'd fixed the tire. "But the beauty of dogma is that it irons out everything. Little 'blips' in our understanding," he said confidently, "become smoothed into a single faith."

"What dogmas do also, however," I pointed out, "is obviate the need for thinking at all. We accept blindly, and anything we accept without thinking by-passes our conscience, and even our sincere understanding."

"Catholic theology, however," Augustus pointed out, "is well reasoned, sound, and unprejudiced."

"*Basically* unprejudiced—except by the need to defend any decree the Church issues," I pointed out. "I'd call that a supreme prejudice. The Church bases its faith on theology, which is to say, on intellectual analysis. The intellect is excellent for analyzing problems, but it is inadequate for arriving at an underlying truth. God can't be analyzed! If He could be, that very fact would make Him subservient to us—as if He were some chemical compound in a test tube! Jesus asked us to love God; he didn't ask us to institutionalize Him. Even when he told Peter, 'on that rock I will build my church,' he was referring to the state of divine realization. By depending too much on intellectual analysis, the Church has objectified his teachings excessively."

"Well," said Brother Augustus, "we don't try to analyze

God. We analyze the godly life and its tenets. Our theology begins with the importance of obedience to God's will, as expressed to us through the Church."

The car was ready to start down the road again. Brother Francis said to me, "Can we continue this discussion after we reach the monastery? I think we'd all be happy to have you join us, and maybe spend the night in our retreat facility." The others both agreed. On the short journey there, I think we were all thinking of questions and answers to the topics under discussion.

The Monks and Obedience

So THEN," SAID BROTHER AUGUSTUS AFTER WE'D arrived at the monastery, and were seated comfortably in a common room, "I was saying that we believe in obedience."

I answered him, "Obedience, yes—to God's will I believe you said. But you qualified your answer by adding, 'as expressed to us through the church.' I believe in obedience to right guidance, but I don't know that I can accept guidance that comes to me merely from someone in authority over me."

"To us," Augustus replied, "obedience to authority means humility before God."

"But if your superiors are wrong—I don't mean on some trivial issue, but on moral or spiritual grounds?"

"We consider it the better part of humility to obey. In this way, we open ourselves more fully to God's will. Of course, if our superiors are wrong, God will correct them, or correct the situation."

"This seems to me a very supine attitude," I said. "It

negates our own discrimination. It means that God must prefer us stupid! To obey mindlessly is to close oneself off from wisdom, not to open oneself to it. Are morons better fit to seek God than mature, intelligent adults?"

"But our superiors know what is for our best. We show our discrimination by doing what they say."

"I can see some benefit in that. Yet I question whether one's superiors really do always know what is best for you. Their first priority is—and has to be—what is best for the organization, not what is best for you. They may feel obliged, for reasons that might benefit the church or the monastery but not necessarily you, to ask you to do something that would be spiritually to your detriment. In this case, obedience to them will weaken both your discrimination and your will power. It will not strengthen you."

"Why should it weaken me?"

"Well, suppose for example that your deep inclination is toward solitude, but your superiors oblige you to travel about the country raising funds for the monastery, won't that be a violation of your spiritual needs? God may be calling you inward, but man, in the form of your superiors, will be forcing you to return to essentially worldly concerns. How can that do anything but stifle the still voice within you which calls, 'Come home!'? In your soul you *know* you should be thinking more of God, but you will deny yourself that inner guidance.

"Or," I continued, "supposing your nature is intensely creative, but your superiors want you to do only what they tell you to do? This, for you, would be suffocating."

"But wouldn't such creativity stem from ego?" Brother Francis chimed in. "Wouldn't it lead to the sin of pride?"

"Not if your creativity were inspired from above and motivated by a desire to help others rather than to shine, personally."

"The sort of person you describe wouldn't be drawn to join our order," Francis concluded.

"I understand," I said. "And please forgive me. I'm not challenging you. Rather, I'm trying to understand things for myself. If I offend, please don't hesitate to say so. My journey has been a quest for understanding—for *self*-understanding. I won't achieve what I'm seeking if I don't question everything. Still, I consider it best to be guided by wisdom, not by human opinion. Reason must show you that. You all are seeking God. Should you not try above all to attune yourselves to *His* ways, rather than to possibly false perceptions of those ways, through others? Human beings are fallible. How can you learn wisdom from them, unless they, too, are wise? You have entered the spiritual path to find God, and not to get caught all over again in limitations. Why be bound to littleness? Your soul wants to expand blissfully into His infinite consciousness."

"I understand what you're saying," said Brother Francis. "I do think it may be better not to surrender my understanding to authority, but only my self-will."

"Well," I said, "that's a beginning. But I don't think it's enough. Superiors are fallible. The pope is fallible. To declare, 'We're all going to march in lock-step togetherness, no matter what,' is surely a mistake. What if you all march in the wrong direction? To me, this sounds positively feudal!"

"We believe, as we told you, that God will set things right for us."

"That's a pious expectation, but I notice that, in the past, the main persecution endured by the saints has come to them from the Church."

"God tests those who love Him."

"Yes, but you'd think the persecution would come more from worldly people than from those who hold basically the same ideals."

"True. But our tests of humility are more likely to come to us from our own people."

"I can see your point."

Brother Francis said. "I think, if ever I'm made a superior, I will allow my subordinates that freedom."

"I don't think I will," said Brother Augustus. "That would encourage the unraveling of monastic discipline."

"Well," I said, "I'm not trying to change your way of life. But I wonder if it is not time for a new kind of monastic system, one in which householders can participate also. If a person is wholly dedicated not only to serving God, but to seeking Him, surely it matters less whether he is married or single. The important thing is that he give all his desires and attachments to God. Otherwise, strict monasticism may lead to pride: humility before one's superiors (even if they are wrong!), but the spiritual pride one can feel in relation to those who haven't embraced such a strict way of life."

Brother Pacificus said, "I rather like your idea. But we're committed, now. It's too late for us to change. Still, I hope things in future will move toward a greater openness. God is beyond anything we can conceive. Too much strictness on our part can lead to fanaticism. I wouldn't want us to become like that. And I wouldn't want us to separate ourselves too far from present-day realities. There has to be a balance, somewhere. I'm glad we met you."

"There's more we can discuss," I said. "Shall we go on?"

"By all means," said Brother Francis, "please do."

We had lunch, then met again for further discussion.

The Monks and Man's Relationship to God

W E WERE OUT OF DOORS, WALKING IN THE
monastery garden. I then broached an even deeper
subject, concerning man's relationship with God.

"I asked you all earlier," I said, "how God made the universe. You answered that we were made by Him. But the
question is, *how* did He make us? He had to make us out of
something. In the past, when man thought of matter as an
irreducible reality, it was natural for a believer not to ponder
this question too deeply. Being impossible to answer, people
decided God just magically produced it all—out of thin air,
so to speak. Now, however, that matter is known to be only a
vibration of energy, we can begin to be more specific in our
understanding. If energy is the underlying reality of matter,
it requires no great leap of thought to say that consciousness
is probably the underlying reality of energy. We know that
will power can control energy. Can we not conclude, then,

that God *projected* Creation, and all of us, out of His consciousness by His will? We are His dreams!"

"That makes sense!" exclaimed Brother Francis with astonishment.

"But then" I continued, "the teaching that Jesus Christ was and is the only son of God cannot be true of him as a man. In his human form, he was no different from us. It had to be in his consciousness that he was the son of God. We are *all* sons of God. The theologians of past centuries had a limited knowledge of objective reality. Their understanding was circumscribed by the paucity of their knowledge. Those were days of relative ignorance."

"So, then," said Brother Augustus, "you are not taking those theologians to task?"

"By no means!" said I. "How could I? They were doing their best with what they had."

"I am glad to hear you say so," replied Augustus. "So many people have challenged them as persons, rather than the realities they had to work with in those days. Even the persecution of Galileo is understandable today, if we look at things from their point of view. Galileo challenged the knowledge of those times. How could they understand that the new methods he used (the telescope) were not simply snares of Satan?"

"Yes, it takes time to change one's ideas. Even scientists often become dogmatically resistant when faced with new discoveries. That is human nature."

"And it is why I accept what you've said," said Francis, "on the point of obedience to wisdom, rather than to authority."

"Now here's another point," I said. "When the Pharisees

accused Jesus of blasphemy for saying, 'I and my father are one,' he answered them, 'Don't your own scriptures say "Ye are gods"?' What he was saying was that we are potentially as great as He! He said that those who believe in him would do what he did. Indeed, he added, '. . . and even greater things.' He didn't come on earth, in other words, to show us how great he was: He came to show us *our own* potential greatness. Back to my first theme: We cannot have been created by God out of nothing. This must mean that He *dreamed* us into existence. He alone is our basic reality! Our destiny, then, can only be to merge back in Him. When Jesus said, 'I and my father are one,' he was holding out that state of oneness as our own true destiny. It is no presumption for us to believe so. Oneness with God is the entire purpose of seeking Him. Our destiny is not an eternity in heaven as the churches teach. Jesus himself used the word, *heaven*, to indicate that state of oneness with God."

"Then why," Augustus challenged, "does the Bible speak of Jesus as the only son of God?"

"But it doesn't. It speaks of *Christ* as the only son. Christ was not the given name of Jesus. It was a title, describing the state of consciousness to which he had attained. He was Jesus *the* Christ. The Christ refers to the highest potential of awareness in ourselves. This alone can have been what Jesus meant when he said we could be like him."

"Then why 'the only son'? Why son, even?"

"The son in a human family," I replied, "is an offshoot of the father: in a sense, a reflection of Him. If God manifested Creation out of His own consciousness, what He manifested had to be a part of Himself. It couldn't be separate from Him. Creation itself is only a vibration of His consciousness. There has to be stillness even at the heart of vibration; otherwise there would be disparity between God, beyond vibration, and His dream. That reflected, unmoving consciousness at the heart of all manifestation is the only begotten Son! Jesus had attained the realization of that aspect of God which is a reflection of the Divine throughout the universe. That is how he could know the thoughts of people from afar. And it is to that state that we, too, must aspire."

"Then the meaning of the Mass," said Brother Francis, "isn't about eating the flesh and drinking the blood of Jesus, the man!"

"Of course not! He wasn't asking us to become cannibals! The ritual of Holy Communion is a reminder of the eternal truth of our own sonship to the Father. In the past, it was virtually impossible to understand this subtle teaching. What Jesus certainly meant in telling his disciples to eat his flesh and drink his blood was that we should commune with the Christ consciousness at the heart of all manifested reality. One might describe that consciousness as flowing through vibration, like blood."

"This is fantastic!" exclaimed Brother Francis. "But I see that the Church couldn't teach these things, given man's understanding in the past. It *had* to be explained away as a 'mystery.' But then, what about the Church's teaching that one needs to be absolved of sin before he may participate in the Mass?"

"Well, didn't Jesus say, 'Blessed are the pure in heart, for they shall see God'? Those words suggest that if we are not pure in heart, we shall *not* see God. Purity of heart means to have no desire except for God. God is eternal Bliss. He is Love. To look for bliss or love where it doesn't exist is to err. And that is all that is meant by sin! To know God, we must be freed from every ripple of bondage to error."

"And that is why we go to confession," said Brother Augustus. "It is to open ourselves completely to God, and to seek perfect purity."

"I agree with that teaching. But do you think it's enough for a priest to absolve you? Moreover, what if your submission to God is more affirmation than actual surrender? Can Jesus himself take your sins if you don't, in your inner heart, give them all to him? Most people only *try* to give themselves to him. Inwardly they continue to cling to their mistakes. The power of habit is very strong."

"Yet the Bible says that Jesus, by his crucifixion, took on the sins of the world," said Brother Augustus.

"And did the world, consequently, become a better place? I don't know that it did. Look at the Roman 'games,' which came centuries later. And consider this: We're supposed to believe that we're free from sin already, but at the same time we're asked to be freed from sin by going to confession. Even confession doesn't do all they claim, for if people really were absolved after confession they would naturally see that sin is error, and abstain from it. In other words, it's really only a ritual, designed to remind people of high truths, but not taking the place of those truths. Absolution by a priest doesn't bestow freedom: it only reminds us of our need for inner freedom."

"My God!" exclaimed Brother Francis. "You're shattering

the very foundations of our belief! And you say you don't want to offend. Yet I see your reasoning, and it's difficult for me to negate it."

"This is why I challenged your vow of obedience. What good results can come from obeying guidance if it is ignorant? It is important for everyone to approach truth with mental clarity. God's reality is the clarity of perfect wakefulness."

"Are you suggesting we leave our monastery, and the Church?"

"By no means! They are good institutions, dedicated to inspiring a holy life. Many good men and women have achieved sainthood through their association with the Catholic Church. And yet, they've done so more because the Church has inspired them to love God than because it has been infallible in its interpretation of the truth. You should take from the Church those teachings which inspire you, but at the same time make your commitment to them one more of heart than of intellect. Love God. As for your monastic vows, chastity is helpful, certainly. It is easier to find God if all one's energy flows toward Him, rather than being divided in obeisance to the world, and to the body. Poverty, or simple living, is a great aid in seeking God, for it frees one from attachment to outwardness. And obedience is essential, provided we give our obedience above all to wisdom and to wise guidance. If we obliterate our own understanding by the obedience we give, we'll never emerge from the cocoon of ignorance."

Brother Francis said, "I see much truth in what you've been saying. But how can we be true to our calling, if we resist what we're taught?"

"I think many saints have faced the same dilemma. How have they remained true to their calling? Simply by accepting that man is fallible, as they themselves are. The Church provides them with a supportive ambience in which they can give themselves entirely to God. You, too, can continue to live inwardly as you've been doing. Just remember why you have chosen this way of life. The kingdom of God, Jesus said, is within you. Live more within. Live deeply for God alone."

"That," said Brother Augustus, "is the real reason we joined the monastery in the first place. To err is indeed human. We don't need to correct things outwardly. And we don't need to change our outer affiliations. We need simply to go more within. Thank you, Brother!"

"And I thank all of you, too," I said. "We can learn much by airing these fundamental issues of faith."

We returned to the monastery. It was time for prayers, and we repaired in silence to the chapel.

ELEVEN

The Monks and the Soul's Journey to God

WE GATHERED THE NEXT DAY AFTER A SIMPLE breakfast. Brother Pacificus began our discussion by blurting out, "I need to know something. How do you account for the differences of natural wisdom? Wisdom can't be genetic. Are the different levels of understanding in mankind simply God's will for us? Surely, according to what you've been saying, we must develop our own understanding."

"Indeed," I answered, "we must learn in everything we do to be co-creators, with Him."

"Still," said Pacificus with a chuckle, "it seems to me we're pretty helpless. An innocent baby is born blind. Or an athlete is permanently crippled in an accident. Co-creators we may be, but it seems to me God throws many obstacles in our path. And I've never been satisfied with the explanation that God's ways are inscrutable. These things have long puzzled me."

"Another thought that has puzzled me in this regard," said Brother Francis, "is, How can the actions of a few years on earth determine our destiny for eternity?"

"Yes," said Pacificus, "how can a finite cause have an infinite effect?"

"We are taught about Purgatory," said Brother Augustus, "but I confess I too have wondered about it all. Is it possible that a few years on earth determine whether we'll live in heaven or hell for eternity? That's a long, long time! If someone goes to hell because he committed murder, two billion years later would God still hold that murder against him? For the murderer himself, the memory of his misdeed must have faded to the point of virtual non-existence! Must his one bad deed remain hovering over him like a cloud forever?"

"I think as you do," I answered. "Besides, what makes one aspiring artist mediocre, and another, excellent? How could Mozart have begun composing symphonies at the age of five? And how can man ever reach the perfection Jesus talked about, when it may take one whole lifetime to overcome even one major flaw in one's nature? Here's a possible answer: Origen, who was considered the greatest early Christian theologian next to St. Augustine, believed in reincarnation. He declared that he'd received this teaching in a direct line of succession from apostolic times. Moreover, the Bible suggests that Jesus himself taught reincarnation."

"Is that so?" they all asked together. "Where?"

"Well, after he was transfigured on the mountain his disciples realized that he was the promised Messiah. They asked him, 'Why then say the scribes that Elias must come first?' And Jesus answered that Elias had indeed come, but people knew him not. The scripture goes on to say the disciples understood that he was speaking of John the Baptist."

My companions were amazed. I went on:

"And when Jesus said to them, 'Who do men say that I am?' they answered that some said he was Jeremiah or one of the other prophets. He couldn't have been one of those old prophets, except as one of their reincarnations. It this was a false teaching, it would have been the duty of Jesus to correct them, yet he didn't."

"Well!" exclaimed Pacificus. "I'm not sure I dare to point that out to my superiors."

"The church," I said, "tried to banish the doctrine of reincarnation from its belief system, because they thought it undermined their threat of eternal damnation for people who didn't toe the line in this life. They anathematized Origen. All this is completely understandable in light of the fact that Christianity developed during an age when no one, anywhere, could see the subtle nature of matter, or the vastness of space. It wasn't until near the end of that age of darkened understanding that people came to realize that the earth is not flat, but round."

"People didn't have all the facts," said Augustus.

"And yet," I remarked, "the evidence was there all the time. At sea, even then, as a ship approached from beyond the horizon, it was visible not as a tiny speck growing gradually larger. Rather, the mast rose up slowly out of the sea; then the hull. The whole ship became fully visible, as it does today, in a matter of moments. People didn't owe their ignorance to the evidence of their senses: they owed it to the fact that they never thought to question. It wasn't evidence they lacked: it was the ability to reason clearly from the evidence, though the facts stared them in the face. The Church, again, is not to blame. But we needn't be bound by past ignorance. It behooves us, in this new age, to study everything anew."

"So then, is a baby born blind because it did something in a former body to attract that punishment?" asked Brother Francis.

"Rather than punishment, why not use the word, 'correction'? Blindness in a baby may be Nature's way of correcting the repeatedly reincarnating ego against a refusal, let us say, to look beyond the beliefs that one holds. Or perhaps, in a former incarnation, that entity put someone's eyes out, and needs to learn that God lives in all bodies, and must be treated with respect everywhere. Whatever energy one puts forth returns in equal measure to oneself. For every action, there is an equal and opposite reaction. That is a Newtonian law. With reincarnation, we can have coherence in life. Not only a chance to keep on growing toward perfection, but also correction when we stray from that path."

"So if a person is born poor," said Pacificus, "it's because he didn't share with others what riches he had in the past?"

"That, or maybe he failed to approach life creatively. Or maybe his first thought, always, was, 'What's in it for me?' Selfish energy is like an eddy, whirling inward contractively to its own center. Poverty is the result of narrow thinking, narrow living, narrow sympathies, narrow expectations of life. It can become a vicious cycle. I once asked a beggar to tell me how to get to some place I was seeking. He turned

away in outrage. To his way of thinking, I ought to be *giving*
to him, not asking of him. I could see he was on a downward
spiral."

"How far downward can one go?" asked Brother Francis.

"The sky is the limit when your goal is infinity. You go on
until you achieve endlessness. This must mean equally that
there are no limits to how far downward you can go."

"Scary!" exclaimed Pacificus.

"Indeed! hardly better than the orthodox hell. But the
soul cannot be destroyed. It is a part of God. Sooner or later,
it must find its way back to its true Source in Infinity."

"That's a beautiful thought," said Francis, "that God is
our Source!"

"Yes, that concept means that, in everything we do, we
should seek inspiration and guidance from our source in
Him, and not only struggle with our own intellects."

"And if God is infinite," said Augustus, "He can't really be
a man. He must be beyond all sexual distinctions."

"Of course! To think of Him in human terms is only a
convenience. 'He' is formless. We must go beyond form if
we would truly become one with Him. You can never really
become one with another person, though men and women
like to think they can, but you *can* merge your formless reality with the formlessness of God."

"This law of action and reaction," said Augustus, "does it
extend to actions of mind as well as of body? If we harbor
resentment against other person, will that person in turn
resent us?"

"That depends on him. He may be beyond feelings of

resentment. But you'll certainly attract resentment from *some* source, in return for the resentment you put out."

"And if we give kindness to others, will others be kind to us?"

"The same answer is true. Individuals may not have advanced to the level where they can express kindness, but you'll certainly get kindness back from life, and from others generally. It is very important, moreover, always to hold positive expectations of life; to be truthful; to be scrupulously honest in our dealings with others; to *want* their best."

"But if every action, every thought, has its consequences, that must mean we pass through many lives before we can reach the perfection Jesus spoke about."

"*Many* lives! I won't even try to guess how many."

"What a grim prospect!" said Pacificus.

"Not really. There's good karma as well as bad. People have fun on the way—fun, as well as pain—happiness balanced by sorrow. Creation itself is founded on the principle of duality: waves rising on the ocean surface, then sinking back again. In time, the sheer repetitiveness of the process becomes anguishing, and the soul longs for release. Meanwhile, as the French say, *L'en s'amuse*: one keeps oneself amused!"

"Then the way of life we've chosen, living for God and renouncing the world, is surely the best way to seek God," commented Brother Augustus.

"It is, in a way, but renunciation must be an inward act. It can't be only an outward penance."

"I must say," admitted Pacificus, "it does sometimes seem

a penance. Chastity, for instance. That's one that many of the Brothers struggle with."

"Of course. The sex instinct is the second strongest in human nature, after self-preservation. Cosmic Nature put it there, to ensure the continuation of the species, and the preservation of the Dream itself!"

"We think of that instinct as a temptation of Satan."

"It is that, too. The satanic force is the divine creative impulse which manifests the Dream. I would go so far as to say that it is primarily the sex drive in man that impels him outward, and keeps him bound to the wheel of reincarnation and to the Dream. You can't suppress that drive. Either you must wholly dedicate yourself to seeking a higher fulfillment, and find a higher bliss to replace it, or you must try mentally to disinvolve yourself from it by impartial introspection, and by withholding mental consent from the act. Negative renunciation isn't enough. There must also be positive, heartfelt dedication. One can live a family life and still be dedicated *inwardly* to that ideal. In some ways family life is easier, unless one is truly ready to give up that attachment altogether. Outward renunciation, moreover, often brings with it the temptation, as I said earlier, to think oneself more spiritual than others—to become proud. Ego is the strongest chain of all!"

"That's what makes our emphasis on humility so important," said Brother Augustus.

"Yes, so long as it doesn't become a new self-definition! You are neither less nor greater than anyone else."

"What, then, is humility?"

"It is forgetfulness of, or indifference to, one's own importance. It means, in all things, seeing God as the Doer. That's why it is wrong to call oneself a sinner. If one is forever grieving over one's sinfulness, and throwing dust on his own head, he is conscious of dust, of his own head, and of his own moral weakness. That kind of humility becomes almost an *excuse* for sinning! I mean, if you really are a sinner, and if that is your self-definition, why not go ahead and sin? Why even pretend you're something better?"

At this, all three of the brothers laughed.

"So tell yourselves," I continued, "I'm a perfect child of God. My sins are only mud covering the gold of my true nature. The more you affirm your potential for perfection, the easier it will be to *achieve* perfection. Whatever you do, feel that you are doing it with God's help. In that way, He will be able to help you more quickly to destroy all the seeds of past karma."

"Thank you very much, Brother," they all said. "You've shown us how to deepen our dedication, and to resolve some of the doubts that naturally arise in the mind of every thinking believer."

"I thank you, also," I said, "for you've helped me, by forcing me to think about them, to appreciate attitudes that I myself have questioned, and have tended to judge uncharitably."

Later, as I set off down the road again, my heart was singing.

TWELVE

Two Saintly Women

I WAS NOW GIVEN AN OPPORTUNITY TO TRAVEL FOR several days without any human encounters. I had been hoping for a few such days, for I wanted to go more deeply in the awareness of God as the Divine Mother, and of my relationship with Her. I felt much bliss coming to me not only from within me, but from Nature. The weather was kind. Sometimes I slept at night in the open fields; sometimes in barns; once or twice at farmhouses where I was welcomed, and had friendly conversations, but no deeply meaningful ones.

One day as I continued down the road I came upon a car stopped by the wayside. The hood was up, indicating engine trouble. Two elderly women were seated calmly inside, evidently waiting for help.

"Can I be of assistance?" I inquired.

"Thank you," they answered smiling. "Our car stopped functioning, and we were waiting for someone to come along who could offer just that. We know nothing about cars. Do you?"

Well, I didn't know much about such things myself, but I looked under the hood and saw that a wire had become disconnected. When I connected it again, the motor worked.

"Have you been waiting here long?" I asked the women.

"Oh, not long," they answered. "Only about an hour."

"An hour! But that's a long time. Weren't you becoming anxious?"

"Not at all," they responded. "We were conversing with our Divine Friend."

"That's how we think of God," the other explained.

"May we offer you a lift?" asked the first one, who was driving.

"I'm very obliged," I said. They were sitting in the front seat, so I got in behind.

"My name's Agnes," said the driver. "And this is my sister, Ella. What is yours?"

"I don't have a name, but you may call me Friend." My anonymity didn't seem to trouble them at all.

"Friend, and Divine Friend!" said Agnes. "How nice."

We set off down the road.

"Will you be going far?" asked Agnes.

"As far as you like," I answered. "I'm on a pilgrimage."

"That's wonderful!" said Ella. "So you, too, love God?"

"I do. And I'm seeking to understand myself that I may love Him even better. I want to cleanse my heart of anything that sings not of God."

"What a lovely way of putting it!" Ella remarked.

We rode some distance in silence. Then Agnes said, "It's about time for lunch. We brought sandwiches, and were thinking of eating them out in the open, under a tree. May we invite you to join us?"

"I'd be grateful," I said.

We went a little further until we came to a large oak tree in a flower-strewn meadow. This seeming to us ideal, we spread out a large blanket and sat there. The women took out several sandwiches from a large basket, a few fruits, cups, and a bottle of water. And there we sat, as well off as we'd have been in any elegant restaurant!

"It's so beautiful in these parts," Agnes said.

"You are not from here, then?" I asked.

"No. We're visiting our brother. The car we're driving belongs to him."

"Where are you from?"

"From Harlem," Ella answered.

"Harlem! You mean, uptown New York City?"

"Yes, that's right."

"Harlem!" I repeated. "It must be very difficult for you to live there."

"No, not at all. Wherever we are, there is our Divine Friend."

"Still, I always think of Harlem as a place of violence and crime."

"It is," Agnes conceded. "But somehow the violence never touches us. We see our Friend everywhere, and everyone treats us in return as a friend."

"One time," said Ella, "a black man came into our little variety shop brandishing a gun. 'Give me your money!' he shouted.

"'Take everything,' we said. 'It's yours anyway. It isn't ours.'

We weren't at all perturbed. Looking around him, he suddenly laughed. 'It isn't much, is it?' he commented. He ended up giving us a hundred dollars!"

Agnes added, "Someone tried bargaining with us over the price of a little alabaster vase. We said to him, 'Please just take it. It's yours anyway.' He ended up giving us more money for it than we'd asked!"

"I suppose," Ella said, "one could call our neighborhood violent, but everyone's always been friendly to us."

"They greet us with smiles," Agnes told me. "But it's true they aren't warm to us. They aren't warm people. I think they feel a little uneasy around us. It's as if they didn't know what to make of us."

"That's interesting," I commented. "It shows that, although they define themselves differently, they know that they too are children of God—taking time out, so to speak, from that reality. What makes them uneasy around you is the fact that you make them feel, deep within themselves, that they need to change. And for now they'd rather go on playing with their little mud pies! Inwardly they are crying, 'We know, we know! But let us play just a little bit longer!' That is how the little self wanders for lifetime after lifetime. Inwardly, however, we all know our true destiny." I paused a moment, then exclaimed with wonder, "What a wonderful show it all is!"

"I think they do know," said Agnes reflectively. "I don't know about our living other lifetimes, but certainly there is something of the divine in everyone—if only people would see it in themselves."

"In some ways," Ella commented, "I'd rather live in Harlem than anywhere else. It keeps us always mindful of the need to hold God in our hearts."

"That reminds me," I said, "of something St. Thérèse of Lisieux said, that if they didn't have a few difficult women in the monastery, it would behoove them to go out, find them, and bring them there."

Both women smiled. Agnes remarked, "Yes, a knife is kept sharp by honing it. Harlem helps us to hone our discrimination and devotion. For that reason, I'm grateful to live there."

"And yet," I added, "you are two very rare souls who have acquired the strength to take only the goodness you see around you. For most people, it would be important to seek a positive, spiritually supportive environment."

"I know you are right," said Ella. "Circumstances tossed us onto that shore, and we've tried to make the best of it. But we've always prayed to God to give us only what we need, to come close to Him."

"Your Divine Friend has given you what is right for you. Someone else He might lead to the safety of a monastic enclosure. Each of us must pray constantly to God, 'Lead me where You want me to go, but never lead me astray!' When Jesus prayed, 'Lead me not into temptation,' I think he was saying that God gives us whatever we ourselves want, and that we should be careful never to want the wrong things— or the wrong directions of development for our own true happiness."

"Yes!" exclaimed Agnes. "It's really a question of people's real happiness. They *think* they'll find happiness in things, but they never do. I think the main thing that puzzles them about us is that we have no personal motives: we only want everybody's welfare. They can only understand people who are motivated by desire, who have some specific goal in life."

"And yet," I said, "those goals are evanescent. As soon as one achieves them, and after gloating a little in the achievement, one discovers that all he has seized is air!"

"It's so nice to realize that we already have, in ourselves, everything we ever sought!" she replied.

"And that," added Ella, "is how we can be contented, even in Harlem. It's a reminder to us that no place, no situation, and no particular thing will ever make us happy. We are happy in ourselves, with our Divine Friend."

We parted later, as their way took them off the road by which I was traveling. They were returning to their brother's home.

"Dear friends," I said to them on parting, "thank you for what you have given me. I see that the most important environment for everyone is God's presence in the heart. An outer environment can help, but the most important thing of all is that we ask Him always to guide us toward Him."

They smiled lovingly, and wished me Godspeed.

THIRTEEN

The Muslim

A CAR STOPPED BESIDE ME. THE DRIVER, A MAN OF swarthy skin, lowered the front window on my side and asked, "Would you like a ride?"

"Thank you," I said, and got in beside him. "What a beautiful day!" I exclaimed.

"*Allah ho akbar!* God is great! God is good!"

"True," I said, "though, when it rains, would we say He is anything less than good?"

"By no means. *Insallah!* Whatever God wills, that is right."

"You are a Muslim?" I inquired.

"Yes," he said. "It is not easy to be a Muslim in this country."

"One meets very few, certainly," I commented. "But I am happy to have the opportunity to meet you, and to discuss religion with you. I think there are misconceptions Christians and Muslims have about each other that might be clarified."

"Well," he replied, "I don't know about misconceptions. God teaches that man should not worship images, but in every Christian church I've entered, I see images of Jesus Christ (on whom be peace), and sometimes of the Virgin Mary and of various saints (peace be on them also). That is going against God's commandment. We accept that Christians believe in God, as we do, but they place images on their altars. That is displeasing to Allah."

"Do you really think Allah can be displeased by anything—that He has such human emotions?"

"Why, certainly He is displeased by wrong action!"

"Well, I won't argue the point. But if an image of Mary makes me love God more deeply, can it be wrong?"

"All right, but the main thing is not God's love, but His will for us. And He wills that we comport ourselves in certain ways. Images are against His commandment."

"His will cannot be whimsical, however. *Why* would images be against it?"

"We are told not to worship any image before Him."

"But if an image serves us as a *reminder* of Him?"

"Images are idols, and idolatry is forbidden by Allah."

"Idolatry means to worship anything that is not of God. To do so is, of course, wrong. As Jesus Christ said, 'Thou shalt love the Lord thy God with all your heart, all your mind, all your soul, and all your strength.' To have an image, however, that inspires is surely very different. It is a *reminder* of Him, and of high spiritual principles. It helps to focus our attention on Him. If we think of Him only in the abstract, how can we know what it is, specifically, that we worship? We should not confuse idol worship with *ideal* worship."

"Well, ideals are not God!"

"They point our way upward, toward Him. They might

be described as rungs on the ladder we must climb to reach Him."

"Well, that makes some sense."

"Even Muslims bow to that sacred stone in the Ka'ba at Mecca. It is inevitable that you should have some symbol. Man needs an outward focus for his attention: an object to remind him of what he is worshiping in the abstract."

"Yes, I see your point," He answered. "Are you saying, then, that the idols even in Hinduism are only images of ideals?"

"What else? Each one represents a quality we need to develop in ourselves. Even beliefs about God are images. But how can we know what He is like with our human minds?"

"Well, of course we can't. Allah is inscrutable."

"Islam, I understand, teaches no higher destiny than that good souls go to heaven. Heaven, however, is a place, a state of being outside of God. This means Muslims believe in a separate reality, apart from God. How can that be?"

"Well, how can anything other than He be a part of Him?" he asked.

"How did anything even come into existence that wasn't a part of Him?"

"Our religion teaches that it did. That is enough for me."

"Still, reason demands that we try to understand, as well as possible, what we are taught. It can't be satisfied with being told to believe blindly."

"When the Holy Quran tells us something is true, and when the Prophet Muhammad (on whom be peace and blessings) declared that this was what the angel Gabriel had taught him, who are we to question?"

"I can see that this belief was possible in an age when people believed that matter is a thing apart from God," I said, thinking of my earlier encounter with Isaac, the atheist. "But how can we take anyone's word for something that today's knowledge shows to be impossible?"

"I can only say that the Holy Quran teaches all men are born pure, and that if we live godly lives we go to heaven. That is better, surely, than the Christian belief that we are born in sin, and that our nature, if unredeemed, will take us to hell."

"I agree with you. And I think that was not the teaching of Jesus Christ. It is what I would call Churchianity, not Christianity."

"In Islam, too, there are sects, and different interpretations of the Holy Quran."

"One thing for which I admire Muslims is their commitment to praying five times a day. It is well, certainly, to remember God always."

"Yes, Muslims are very devout."

"Another thing which I admire in you is how you submit everything to the will of God."

"That, too, is a feature of Islam."

"I question, however, your insistence that the ways of serving Allah can be so severely regulated. There are so many human realities. It is like many paths up a single mountain. It is enough, surely, that we move in a generally upward direction. When people insist too much on outer rules, they become rigid and self-righteous. They also come to equate piety itself with such rigidity. This tendency to tell other people how to live is, it seems to me, a weakness in all the Semitic religions: brittle fundamentalism."

"I think it is also a weakness in human nature," he commented. "When we focus on other people's faults, we worry less about our own."

"You're absolutely right," I said. "And the funny thing is, it isn't by worrying about our own faults, either, that we can achieve inner freedom. It is by concentrating on the perfection of God's bliss. The other way leads to the concept of jihad—of holy war."

"Jihad, in Islam," he replied, "does not mean holy war. It means struggle. That struggle is individual. It means the struggle to live a godly life."

"Yet too often it has meant suppressing others. History shows vast conquests and conversions to Islam by the sword. If that isn't holy war, I don't know what you mean by the term."

"We are mostly pacific people," he said. "But some of us, I admit, have interpreted jihad differently."

"Yes, and although there are lamentably many Christian fundamentalists, too, at least they don't go launching large bomb attacks on innocent people in the name of their beliefs."

"Yes, Muslim terrorists are an embarrassment to the rest of us. They have caused much misunderstanding about our religion."

"Jihad seems also to include the principle of defending your religion. This practice has led not only to aggressive conversion and terrorism, but also to denying other people the freedom to follow their own practices—for example, in ancient places like the pyramids. Friends of mine who have tried to meditate in the 'King's Chamber' of the great pyramid have had Muslims shout in their faces to stop them from doing so."

"I am sad to hear that. It should not be so. Islam is a very tolerant and rational religion."

"I have also read some of the life of Muhammad . . ."

"The Prophet, on whom be peace and blessings."

"As you say, but in some of what I've read he doesn't come across as a peaceful or gentle person at all."

"Well, what can one say? Those were difficult times."

"Muhammad," I thought, but didn't say, "was born almost at the lowest point of Kali Yuga, the dark age. Yes, those *were* difficult times!" Out loud I said, "I do know there have been saints in Islam. Rabi'ah was one. So also seem to have been Rumi and Omar Khayyam."

"Yes. They were Sufis. Not all Muslims approve of that sect, but it seems to include saintly people."

"Omar Khayyam wrote in one quatrain, according to Fitzgerald's translation:

Up from Earth's Centre through the Seventh Gate
I rose, and on the Throne of Saturn sate,
And many Knots unravel'd by the Road;
But not the Knot of Human Death and Fate.

"This quatrain, and many others, suggest a very mystic insight into spiritual truth."

"That is not a teaching I know," he commented. "Still, I cannot argue the point."

"I would like to learn from you," I said. "I'm not trying to be critical. I must add that I consider myself rather spiritual than religious in my inclinations. What impresses me most in what you've said is that the people of your faith believe in complete surrender to the will of God. *Insallah!* Yes, if we truly seek God's will in all things, everything must come out for the best, eventually, in our lives."

"You are, I can see, a well-meaning person. If we can all live together in harmony on this earth, Allah will, I believe, be well served."

"The trouble is," I said, "that the harmony so many of you envision is a harmony under Islam. Even if all the world were converted to your religion, that would be no guarantee that the world would then become peaceful. Just look at the warfare that exists even now between the different interpreters of the Quran."

"Yes, I'm afraid warfare is part of human nature."

"I think we must recognize its reality in ourselves, and resolve for our own peace of mind to be peaceful and loving to all. To me, the valid message of Islam is that I must proclaim jihad against my own lower self. Unless and until I unite my own being in one upward aspiration toward God—or, if you like, toward Allah—I'll never know inner peace."

"On that point, I believe we are agreed."

"But," I added, "I'm afraid your fundamentalists are sowing the karmic seeds of their own destruction. We shall see. What you believe is, I believe, bound to become absorbed in a broader vision of the divine truth."

"As you said, 'We shall see.'"

And so, with mutual expressions of good will, we parted.

FOURTEEN

The Lawyer

SPENT THAT NIGHT QUITE COMFORTABLY IN AN OPEN field. The next morning I washed in a crystal-clear brook, and breakfasted adequately on a few berries. *Insallah!* I thought. Everything in life is as it should be!

I then set off down the road again. I had proceeded some distance when a very expensive-looking car stopped beside me. Again came the question: "Would you like a ride?" It was a well-dressed man this time, efficient looking and speaking somewhat loudly.

"Thank you," I replied, and got in the front.

"What's your name?" the man asked.

"I'm trying to forget it," I answered. "You may just call me Friend."

"In trouble, eh? I wonder if I could help you? I'm a lawyer. Name's Williams."

"A lawyer, are you? What kind of law do you practice?"

"All kinds. In these economic times, it's better not to specialize."

"Well, let me begin by saying, No, I'm not in any trouble. I'm not on the lam, and I don't need a lawyer. I'm on a spiritual quest for understanding, and I want to put self-definitions behind me. Who I am in God's eyes, after all, has nothing to do with my name, occupation, country, or anything else. Self-definitions are like prisons in which we incarcerate ourselves."

"I, on the other hand, deal in definitions of all kinds, including self-definitions. I must consider questions like, 'Are you guilty or not guilty? Can you afford to pay me? What did you do wrong? What did your wife do wrong? What did others do to you that was wrong? Where were you at eight o'clock on the night of the eighteenth of September?' I have to pin people down, and get them to tell as many specifics about themselves as possible. We couldn't be in more diverse professions, if you'd call what you do that!"

"That difference may give us a chance to understand even ourselves—our 'professions,' as you say—in new ways," was my comment.

"Intriguing answer," he said. "Tell me, have you ever been to court?"

"Only on the tennis court. I lost, but I'm trying to forget that, too!"

"Well, believe it or not as you will, but most Americans are unbelievably litigious. They'll sue you if you so much as step onto their property; spill coffee on their clothes; or call them unpleasant names—even if they deserve to be called much worse! And married couples! You should see them fight! We lawyers get called in for everything."

"You seem to be thriving, financially."

"Well, I can't complain. But there's plenty of competition. No country on earth has anything like the number of lawyers we have in America."

"Tell me something. I've often wondered: Is your concern more with the truth? or is it with winning?"

"Well, I'm hired to win, am I not?"

"So, then, if you happen to know a truth that would be prejudicial to your client's case, do you hide it?"

"Well, naturally! I let my opponent find it, if he sniffs the possibility and decides to ferret it out."

"Do you color the truth in a client's favor? For instance, if he or she is obviously guilty, do you try to make him seem innocent?"

"Well, that's my job. Actual guilt or innocence is for the judge to decide."

"And do you try to make an opposing client look bad, even if you know he's not bad at all?"

"Well, that too is my job."

"I see. So you're willing to bend the truth, when necessary?"

"Well, I don't think of it that way, but of course I must tip things in my client's favor when I can."

"Look, we've been discussing your self-definition as a lawyer. But what about you as a man? Doesn't this tendency to bend the truth affect you in your personal life as well?"

"I don't believe so."

"No? Would you never lie to your wife?"

"Well, sometimes what she doesn't know won't hurt her. If I put money on a horse, for instance, and it loses, why should I tell her about it?"

"And what if you came home late because you visited friends she doesn't like, would you tell her you'd had to stay late at the office?"

"Well, a little white lie like that wouldn't hurt her. Otherwise, well, I can imagine the storm!"

"What if you met an old girlfriend. Would you hide that fact from your wife?"

"Just a minute! You're questioning me like a lawyer, yourself!"

"But I'm trying to ascertain, for your sake, the depth of your commitment to the truth. It seems to me a bit shallow."

"What do you mean, for my sake?"

"Well, when we are truthful, we have support from reality itself—from the universe, if you will. And with that support, everything will always come out for the best. But without it, things cannot but fall apart, sooner or later. People cease to trust us. People cheat us, as we've cheated them. Things we counted on let us down at crucial moments. We lose friends, and find ourselves with none to support us but those for whom we ourselves have no respect. Nothing works when we don't tell the truth. And when we are truthful, everything we do in life flourishes."

"That sounds like a pleasant fairy tale."

"But imagine a lawyer who is strictly truthful with his clients; who won't accept a case if he doesn't believe in it; who tries honestly to see both sides, and offers his services on the strength of his knowledge of the law, but who doesn't try to find ways of bending the law in his client's favor. Such a man will gain a reputation for complete integrity. In time, judges themselves will be biased in favor of any case he represents. Such a lawyer, surely, will be more successful, even if it takes him time to become so."

"Well, I know of no lawyers like that, so I can't comment. As far as I'm concerned, the truth is relative. A lawyer might as well be realistic. Anyway, how can one ever be sure in his own mind whether the case he accepts is valid or not? We lawyers leave it to the courts to decide that issue. As I said, truth is for the judges to decide. As for us, meanwhile, we are like hired guns."

"Sort of intellectual goons, in other words?"

"Well, I wouldn't put it that strongly."

"Still, integrity is less important to you than winning. Forgive me. I do seem to be in a very different profession from yours. My own is a quest for self-understanding. I have to say that if I were threatened even with bankruptcy, I would never sacrifice my self-respect. That is how strongly I believe that lasting success of any kind depends on right action. Were I to tell lies, someday I'd reach the point where I didn't even know what was or was not right action."

"Does it matter all that much, so long as you win?"

"To me it does. I firmly believe that even the willingness to indulge occasionally in a wrong act will lead, in the end, to either failure or a complete loss of self-worth. I'd say that the worst failure of all was the loss of my own integrity. Money in the bank is trivial by comparison."

"Well, I'd call you an extremist. Everyone I know in my profession behaves as I do."

"And are any of you happy?"

"What's that got to do with it? But yes, I guess I could say I'm happy."

"What you mean is, you're not miserable, and your income keeps you afloat enough not to want to commit suicide."

"Well, that's a novel way of putting it! But I guess what I really mean is, no, I'm not completely happy yet, but I'm on the road to happiness."

"Which is always receding from your grasp! I do know what you mean. You're too numb really to think about it, for now. The underlying motive behind everything most people do is the urge for happiness. And you're always short by just inches of finding it."

"Are you saying my first criterion, in every decision I make, should be whether an act will lead me to increased happiness?"

"That's exactly what I'm saying."

"So if a client comes to me because he wants to sue for divorce, I should ask myself, 'Will it make me happy to take this case?'"

"No, you should ask yourself, 'Will divorce be the best thing for my client? Would he and his wife be happier if they could find some way to reconcile their differences?' You might then try to bring about that reconciliation."

"And lose a potential client! I must say, that doesn't sound very practical! Surely the decision as to whether they get divorced is their own."

"But you'd be much happier in yourself if you could bring about a reconciliation between them. Moreover, you might find that you'd opened up a new career for yourself—as a mediator. And you would find yourself drawing more and more of the right sort of clients. The best publicity a lawyer can have is by word of mouth."

"I can see some truth in what you're saying," conceded Mr. Williams a little reluctantly. "Still, to survive in this practical world, I think everyone has to cut corners occasionally."

"I've been speaking in a sort of 'push-me-pull-you' manner that you might find easier to understand: If I do so-and-so to you, you'll do the same to me. But the matter really goes much deeper. For example, if you always abide strictly by the truth, you'll find yourself able, in time, to come up with new solutions to problems. You'll find new and better ways of achieving your goals. You'll understand obscure difficulties effortlessly, which, for you, won't even seem as difficult as they once did."

"Really! Now, that thought sounds worth pursuing."

"Not only that," I said. "You'll find that you can make what you want happen in ways that, to other people, may seem miraculous. The reason for your success will be that you'll find yourself in tune with the universe. If you want to master a subject, you'll find yourself able to do so without effort. If you find yourself wishing something would happen—incredibly, it happens! If you wish to understand things, amazingly again, you'll suddenly find that you do understand them. And all this will be easy to achieve, simply because you put yourself in tune with what *is*, instead of trying to manifest what isn't."

"You mean, if I play the stock market, I'll win?" Mr. Williams suddenly seemed a little more hopeful that what I was saying might be true.

"Well, yes—you'll win, up to a point. But greed will soon disturb your attunement with the truth. Truthfulness means much more than adhering to the facts. It means attunement with a higher reality. By selfishness, you will separate yourself from broader realities of which you are a part."

"You mean—oh, this is a little hard to swallow! How can I be a part of everything? I'm me, Roger Williams. I'm not some sort of mist!"

"Roger Williams is really only a wave on the great ocean of reality."

"A wave, eh? And you're another one? How come we're so different?"

"Our shapes are different, but the one ocean beneath us is our underlying reality. The more we recognize it, and don't try to separate ourselves from it by trying to tower over other waves, the greater our own peace. Metaphors, however, are never adequate. What I'm saying also is, by attunement with the ocean of wisdom we ourselves become wise. And by trying to be important in ourselves we separate ourselves to a greater or lesser extent from recognition of the abiding reality of that ocean. Thereby, we lose in the end not only our clarity, but our happiness."

"Well, I have to say you're presenting me with an altogether new picture of reality. Maybe I'll give a thought to trying what you've said."

"But I should caution you: If you follow what I say, you won't find things always working out as you wanted. You'll only find them working out for your best, and for your *true* happiness. If you try to do something that isn't in tune with higher reality, the universe will work against you."

"Well," he remarked with a gesture of comic hopelessness, "it seems there's a catch to everything!"

"It isn't really a catch, though. It's true that adherence

to truth may actually bring you suffering—for example, the pain of loss. But that's because strict truthfulness is an upward flow toward perfection. Anything in your nature that clings narrowly to your ego must be purged. You'll reach the point where the process is not even painful any longer. You'll accept it unflinchingly—and even with joy."

"And you've tested these principles? You've found they actually work."

"I have. And they do. But," and here I paused, "please forgive me! I've been working these things out for myself. What I've been saying is far beyond anything I'd ask of you. Mr. Williams, if you will simply try to align your actions with truth, I know you'll find the happiness that's been eluding you so far."

"I like what you've been saying," he remarked with an expression of gratitude. "I'm going to give it serious thought. Wow! My wife won't recognize me!"

I smiled.

FIFTEEN

Two Artists

TWO PEOPLE WERE SEATED IN THE FRONT OF THE next car that picked me up. The driver was a man; beside him sat a woman.

"I wonder," began the man shortly after I'd made myself comfortable in the back seat, "if you can comment on a discussion we've been having. What do you think of Picasso?"

"As a man?" I asked, "or as an artist?"

"Well, both."

"As a man, he seems to have had an engaging sense of humor. Once, when a woman showed him a Picasso painting, he said, 'It's a fake.' 'But it bears your signature,' she protested. 'Well,' Picasso replied, 'I can paint a fake Picasso as well as anyone else.'"

"Yes," agreed the man with a smile. "And another time Picasso offered people a new painting without comment, just to see what people thought of it. They, hypnotized as they were by his fame, raved over it. At the height of its acclaim, he announced, 'It was painted by my pet monkey.' That, too, shows a good sense of humor."

We all three laughed appreciatively.

"On the other hand," said his wife, "I don't think much of him as an artist. And even as a man, his morals were far from ideal."

"Moreover," I said, "he was a communist. That isn't a comment on his morals, but it does say something about his lack of discrimination."

"I wonder," said the man, "whether he wasn't just trying to shock people by that affiliation. The artist Salvador Dali said of him, 'Picasso is a painter, so am I; Picasso is a Spaniard, so am I; Picasso is a communist, neither am I.' I suspect he wasn't really dedicated to any cause. One might call him an armchair communist."

"You know," said I, "I think the reason his paintings appeal to so many people is not their artistry, but their shock value."

"We were just saying the same thing," said the woman.

"Art in the twentieth century," I commented, "whether paintings, or sculptures, or music, or poetry—and even much of the literature in prose—seems like a boat adrift without a rudder. Ultimately, everything one does reflects one's outlook on life. If one's outlook is fractured or negative, his art will reveal that fact. Art cannot exist in a vacuum."

"What do you think of the various 'isms' in art: cubism, surrealism, impressionism, and the rest? Are you especially drawn to any of them?"

"Well," I replied, "what I said applies to all art. It isn't the 'isms' that matter so much as the consciousness behind a particular work. But among the 'isms,' I suppose I like impressionism the best because at least it expresses more deliberately the artist's consciousness. Other works pretend not to, but fail in the effort because the way the artist views things cannot help coloring everything he does. Yes, 'colors' is a good word here. A pessimistic artist who styles himself a realist will inevitably choose even colors that express his pessimism."

The man said, "I think you're right. By the way," he said, interrupting himself, "my name is Ron. This is my wife, Betty."

"It's nice to meet you both," I replied. "You may call me Friend, though in fact I wasn't named that at birth."

"A sort of *nom de plume*, eh? You must be an artist or a writer, like ourselves. I'm a painter. Betty is a composer. Artists often have professional names. Well, Friend, have you any thoughts on what we've been talking about?"

"I have often thought about these things," I said. "It seems to me that no one can have a completely original idea. Our thoughts are reflections of states of consciousness, which are simply 'out there.' An individual's thoughts reveal his own level of consciousness. A sensual person will reflect thoughts that arise from a lower level of consciousness. A saint will reflect the thoughts that emanate from an uplifted awareness. But the brain doesn't *produce* ideas: it can only *transmit* them.

"Most people," I continued, "are strongly affected by the thoughts that prevail during the age in which they live. If those thoughts are negative and permeated with spiritual doubt, people's thinking will be negative and full of doubts also. They won't think that way merely because it's stylish to do so: that style itself will seem to them perfectly right and natural.

"Therefore," I added, "it is wise to keep oneself somewhat separate from the general attitudes of one's times."

"What an intriguing concept!" said Ron. "We artists pride ourselves on being independent thinkers, but I do notice that fads spring up in the arts, and that for artists to think alike in certain ways seems sort of *de rigueur.*"

"Exactly. So we shouldn't blame *them* if they are mistaken. In fact, there's no need to blame anyone at all. We only need to understand where they are coming from. Some thoughts and attitudes, however, lead to greater wisdom, whereas others lead to a lessening of wisdom. We need to select for ourselves, without blaming anyone, the upward road to ever greater understanding. And that usually means resisting fads and faddish influences. Indeed, most people are committed only to various levels of ignorance!"

"So how do you suppose all these artistic 'isms' got their start? There have been so many of them in modern times. In the past, people simply painted what they considered to be art, without concocting elaborate theories as to what art ought to be."

"I think," I said, "it's because we've entered a new age of energy. There's a sort of tug-of-war, now, between the old ways of thinking—which depended on seeing matter as real and permanent—and new ways, which see life in more fluid terms. The nineteenth century saw the dawn of this new awareness of energy, and resisted it rigidly. It clung with newly awakened *energy* to the view that everything was forever fixed and material. One scientist declared, 'If you can't show me a working model of your ideas, I cannot accept them.' As the twentieth century dawned, people went to the opposite extreme of doubting that *any* fixed verities existed anywhere. And so those people, including artists, who thought at all about life and meaning decided that everything was relative, and that nothing was absolute. Values, they declared, are purely subjective. And they came to the same conclusion regarding questions of right and wrong. The arts merely reflected the prevailing belief that life has no meaning. In every field of artistic expression, there was confusion—indeed, chaos. Every artist who tuned in to that consciousness reflected it in his art. Picasso was simply a good example of the trend, and many people, swayed by this widespread belief, accepted and even acclaimed his work."

"Picasso," Betty pointed out, "was also a communist. Would you call that system, too, just another fad?"

"Of course it is. One might call it the dying gasp of man's addiction to rigid materialism! It is a religion, virtually, of materialism: even more fixed and rigid than the system of aristocracy that prevailed during the feudal age—a system that was based on the solid-seeming reality of land ownership. But that system gave way to rule by the people, and communism ossified it still further into a system dictated by the lowest human values, not the highest. This led naturally to a Godless society, since the system itself was essentially mindless. Communism is the quintessential religion of materialism. Inevitably it chose for its symbol a lower image: the hammer and sickle, which represented manual as opposed to intellectual labor, and spoke for the lowest type of humanity: people who hardly think at all, but who merely plod through life like cows and oxen! To that new and far-from enlightened way of thinking, these people represented the very opposite aspect of human nature from that part which raises man to the heights. It was simply because people didn't equate those heights with greater energy and understanding, but only with physical force."

"And that gave rise to further delusions!" interjected Betty.

"Well, naturally. Those who were bright enough to understand the potentials this system held for mass control tried to exert power over the 'unthinking masses.' People with the brains to see through this folly sought to control those who embraced it. Communists don't really believe in the equality of all men: they believe in a new kind of aristocracy, an aristocracy of power. Naturally they have a dislike for intellectuals. And *naturally* they purged them! Picasso, himself an intellectual, was told by the surrealist André Breton, 'I don't approve of your joining the Communist Party, nor with the stand you have taken concerning the purges of the intellectuals after the Liberation.' He refused, therefore, even to shake hands with Picasso.

"Yet those purges, too, were inevitable, given the development of people's thinking under that system. Their atheism was inevitable. And what appears to be the madness in modern art is equally inevitable. These are all thoughts spun like cotton on a woof of inevitable action and reaction. A person can be understanding, and even forgiving, when he removes himself from fad-consciousness, and seeks his inspirations from God.

"The first thing we must do," I continued, "is remove our awareness from ego-consciousness: get rid of this delusion that we create our own ideas! We cannot create them. We can only reflect ideas that exist already."

"Wow!" said Ron. "Then art is process of selecting the level from which we'd like to draw our inspiration."

"Exactly," I said. "Art ought also, therefore, to inspire. The philosophy, 'Art for art's sake,' is a sham. Art cannot but express a particular outlook on life, and that outlook ought to be uplifting. If its influence is debasing, then it betrays its own high mission."

"And yet," said Betty, "art, to be true art, must also be subtle. It can't be obvious about its calling. It should inspire by being, not by preaching. It's message should not *seem* to be a message: it should only express states of consciousness that, in themselves, are inspiring."

"Yes," said Ron. "A painting of a mountain peak, let's say, should not overtly state (for example), 'This peak is a symbol of the upward climb to perfection.' It is enough if the artist feels inspiration in the thought of such a climb. His painting then will inevitably convey upward aspiration."

"I think you've expressed it beautifully," I said. "An artist who feels inspired will naturally convey something of his inspiration to others in everything he does. He doesn't have to be a missionary. Even the colors he chooses will suggest aspiration. His lines will be harmonious, not jagged. He will show complete human beings, not (as Picasso did) schizo-phrenics. And even the schizophrenics he painted were only reflections of a widespread philosophy of life, suggested by Freud, who in turn was influenced by the bottom-upward thinking of his age. Picasso, in his very rebellion against convention, was merely a creature of his times, reflecting its values and its outlook on life. That is why I say we should resist the spirit of the times in which we live. We should be centered in our own inner reality. We shouldn't let mere opinion rule our sense of what *is* truly fitting, regardless how socially prevalent those opinions are. Mostly they reflect only passing fads."

"What about music?" asked Betty. "I'm a composer. It seems to me that in this field, too, there has been a great deal of confusion. Beautiful melodies seem almost a thing of the past. So-called classical music, especially, gives the impression of almost taking pride in its lack of melodic sense. Think of Stravinsky's 'The Rite of Spring'! It's as if composers—who ought in a sense to be philosophers—wanted to make mankind out to be constructed like mindless machines! Harmonies are deliberately disturbing, reflecting an attitude of nervous distrust of the universe and of everyone in it. And the rhythms! Their heavy downbeat, as if affirming self-importance; their irregularity, as if to shock and disorient. A little syncopation brings in the unexpected and keeps things lively, but too much of it tosses a person about mentally, like a rag doll in a clothes washing machine! Where is all this leading? So far, it seems as though composers wanted deliberately to disturb everybody's nerves!"

"And meaninglessness in the visual arts," I said, "has reached a point where people feel they can call any system of pipes a work of art just because they, the 'artists,' label them so. I hope" I added, "that we're coming out of that period. Meaning is not subjective. We are all linked together in a great web of reality. That is truly meaningful for everyone which takes people closer to where they themselves want to be. And all they really want is one thing: bliss. Because many people reject the idea of God, most of them translate their desire for bliss into a search for happiness. Still, can those pipes, can schizophrenic faces, can jangled rhythms, can melodies that are completely lacking in all aspiration—can any of these give anyone what everyone on earth really wants: happiness? In time, people will come to understand—each one in his own time—that happiness itself is only a lower octave of bliss."

"Yet the aspiration for happiness is completely missing from modern visual art and music. The vibration is often heavy, self-affirming, even angry."

"Yes," I replied, "as you suggested Betty, the first beat of every measure of music represents the ego. 'From here,' it says. 'I will act.' When that beat is strong, it is impossible to convey a sense of happiness or upliftment, for the ego is the source of all our misery! Think of rock 'n' roll music, especially. People feel excited by it, but excitement is not happiness. Indeed, in peacelessness there can be only misery. People hope, by letting themselves get excited, to forget themselves, but they only delude themselves. Always, what they affirm in their excitement is the thought, *'I'm* excited!' Excitement erects a wall around their egos, enclosing them inside it. It also exhausts people, leaving them more dissatisfied than ever. That is why so many people who are addicted to this form of so-called 'music' are angry with the world. They campaign angrily for a change. They protest against what they perceive as injustice, but their attention is focused on what is wrong with the world, because they are wrong in themselves. Otherwise, they would be at peace, and would know that life itself is only the manifestation of the heaving movement of waves on the great ocean of reality. Underlying all of life there should be the calm faith that God knows what is best for us, and will guide us steadily toward His bliss. But how can there be faith, or even calmness, when one has no values? The only way to create good art these days is to protect oneself from the influences everywhere around us: symptoms, as I said, of a shift in consciousness into that of a new age. Art *can* help with this transition, by tuning in to and inspiring people with these new rays. But for art to accomplish this, the artist himself needs to have some wisdom. He also needs to accept that few people, for now, will understand the value of his contribution. That appreciation will come, probably long after his death."

"It's amazing," Betty said, "how music, especially, reflects states of consciousness. The discord of modern 'harmonies' demonstrates people's lack of faith in higher values, and in themselves. It reveals a lack of harmony in their own lives."

"A few discords," I said, "may help to show that we know ourselves to be creatures of a higher destiny than anyone can predict. Constant discord, however, suggests a state of being that is totally out of control, like a car with failed brakes, careening downhill toward inevitable disaster!"

"So, then," said Betty, "the first thing an artist or a composer must do is develop himself as a human being. Whatever he expresses will be a manifestation of who he is, inwardly. If he wants to produce worthwhile art, he must first become a worthwhile person. He simply cannot go with the crowd."

"I think," I said, "that an artist must train himself to think in terms of what pleases his higher self. He should never struggle for popularity. It is better even to be poor than to ignore one's own conscience by making his priority in life the accumulation of money."

"What subjects should an artist choose to paint," asked Ron, "in order to express meaning? We've exhausted by now the old themes that conveyed inspiration in traditional ways: Jesus, Mary, the saints. Paintings of staid burghers may show skill, but for beauty, what do those portraits offer us? Pictures of people, whether individually or in crowds, however well the paintings may be executed, don't necessarily uplift."

"I think the *theme* is less important than the consciousness behind it. A work of art conveys, above everything else, vibrations of consciousness. If the artist looks at a beautiful landscape with a happy attitude, he will convey a sense of happiness when he paints it. He could show a harmony between man and Nature. Think, in this respect, of the paintings of Watteau. Each artist will be, and should be, himself. I think, however, that the best way to express higher states of consciousness is not through Natural beauty, but in the human face and figure. After all, a tree has not, in itself, a highly developed consciousness. Only man expresses consciousness overtly. And only man can express *refined* states of consciousness. I think the highest form of art requires human beings for models.

"Why not show people," I continued, "feeling inspired, or filled with faith in God, or expressing selfless love for one another? I admit it is *easier* to show emotions like anger, or selfishness, smugness, pride, and the like. Caricatures, being distortions, are easier to make believable. Moreover, it is more difficult to show noble qualities. But what will inspire people and make them look at a work of art again and again? Always, they will be drawn to a painting if it inspires them—especially if the inspiration they feel from it awakens in them a desire to become better human beings themselves. Restless people may turn away from such art, but ultimately the goal of art must be to satisfy both the artist and the soul of man."

"And the same is true for music," said Betty.

"Yes. That which satisfies the composer will stand the greatest chance, in the end, of satisfying others also. The French have a saying: *'Tout comprendre c'est tout pardonner*—to understand all is to forgive all.' But I don't see that there is anything, anywhere, to forgive. Indeed, forgiving implies a sense of superiority! I would say, rather, that to understand all is to accept the right of everyone simply to be himself. Where is the need to criticize? Criticism is justified only if one is using discrimination to find the right values for himself. It should never be leveled against individuals. Everyone has a right to come at truth in his own way, at his own time, and according to his own level of understanding."

"Well," said Ron, "I'm happy we picked you up! You've clarified many things for us."

"Yes," said Betty, "this has been a wonderful discussion."

"It has helped me, too," I said, "for it has directed my attention to the importance of being *self*-directed in my life. Moreover," I added, "though I've spoken of historic influences on our thought, I wonder sometimes if we are not influenced also by cosmic currents of consciousness, far beyond the confines of this little planet. For everything is composed of consciousness. The whole universe seems like a dream in the mind of the Creator. The only way to get away from all objective influences is to seek attunement with our Creator. In that way alone can we waken from the dream.

"And the highest purpose of art," I added, "is to help people to awaken from the dream. Art can do so more easily when it helps to raise people's consciousness out of the mud of sensory addiction. The arts reach us through the senses, but it isn't by denying ourselves sensory enjoyment that we can rise above it: it's by *refining* our enjoyment. Not by turning away from a beautiful sunset with a yawn, but by enjoying it *inwardly*, with the joy of the soul, can we become uplifted in God's joy."

"The arts, then," said Betty, "can and should be an great aid to religion. In that sense, artists have a holy mission. They should not trivialize that mission even by depicting things that are pleasant but of no consequence."

"This, I believe," I said, "is the essence of what good art should accomplish. It should be something one can introduce into one's home as a friend, even as a counselor who is wise, insightful, and inspiring."

SIXTEEN

The Evolutionist

I TRAVELED FOR SEVERAL DAYS WITHOUT ANY SPECIALLY meaningful encounters. I think I gained something from all of them, but I consider none worth recording in the pages of this book. I made progress, however, toward my eventual goal, which was in Mexico City. The Basilica of Guadalupe contains the icon of the famous Patroness, or Divine Mother, of all the Americas.

I was walking one day in a southerly direction, when a car stopped beside me. Asked the usual question, I responded with thanks and got in, sitting in front with the driver. He was a man over sixty, well dressed and dignified.

"I was wanting company," he said. "Where are you headed?"

"Mexico City," I replied.

"That's a long way," he commented. "May I ask why you're traveling so far by foot?"

"I'm on a pilgrimage," I answered.

"A pilgrimage!" he exclaimed. "Now, why would you be going to Mexico City of all places?"

"The shrine of Our Lady of Guadalupe is there."

"Forgive me. You look intelligent and well educated. But how can you believe in shrines, and in persons who aren't there, and in things that defy all logic? Really, I don't want to offend, but how can you be so credulous? As I said, you look like a sensible man. What's all this about a pilgrimage? It strikes me as slightly unbalanced!"

"I'm on a quest for self-understanding."

"But what's there to understand? You're a mass of whirling electrons, of billions of molecules. Our job, as reasoning human beings, is to understand as much as we can about the world and the universe around us."

"I'd say it's important also to understand why we're here; what life is all about. That, partly, is why I'm on this quest."

"Well, Darwin made it clear that man evolved by accident. There is no meaning behind evolution: it just happened."

"You mean that low forms only blundered upon higher forms?"

"Essentially, yes. It was a question of survival of the fittest: Those who were fitter to survive produced more offspring; these in turn were more fit to survive; and so they became dominant species."

"Was there no intelligence in the process?"

"No, it was all mechanical—quite meaningless. Life evolved more or less just because it was there to happen."

"So human intelligence evolved just because the intelligence of human beings made them better able to survive?"

"That's right."

"Why, then," I asked, "are human beings so much more intelligent than other creatures? If survival were the only issue, and man's intelligence is the particular gift that enabled him to survive, then surely it would suffice for man to be only a little more intelligent than other creatures."

"Well," he replied, "you have a point. Maybe he needed to improve his intelligence so as to survive competitively against other human beings!"

"Yet we see that all human beings have more or less the same degree of awareness. It has been said that man uses only ten percent of his potential brain power. This suggests that man has reached a level of evolution where his faculties can be developed for their own sake, and not in competition with other human beings."

"But in any case, man just appeared on the scene. How can matters have been otherwise?"

"Well, *why* did higher and higher forms evolve, up to the human level?"

"Why label them higher, anyway? Can we say that man has evolved more in producing a brain than an elephant has, in producing a trunk?"

"Isn't it obvious," I asked, "that consciousness is higher than a mere physical appendage?"

"Not to me, it isn't. Everything is material in the end, anyway." (Shades of the logic offered me by the atheist I'd met, days earlier!) I came back at him, as I had at Isaac, with the example of the earthworm. I showed him how an earthworm, though not intelligent as we human beings would define the word, is yet self-conscious, and is also capable of feeling: two things, I said, that science will never be able to replicate. But then I added,

"Earthworms have survived for countless millions, maybe

billions, of years. What caused life to produce higher and higher forms, as I call them? Wouldn't the earthworm have sufficed?"

"Darwin explained it all by the simple process of mutation: accidents, in other words. Sports of Nature."

"Most mutations," I said, "are disadvantageous. A cow with five legs: that sort of thing."

"Yes, but some mutations aren't. And it is to those occasional successes that we owe the whole evolutionary process. Consciousness has nothing to do with it. If a leopard in the jungle is born without spots, it is evolutionally at a disadvantage compared to the spotted breed. The unspotted leopard is less suited to survive in the jungle, and therefore less likely to survive. Thus, survival is biased in favor of the spotted variety, and spots eventually prevail. Leopards with spots are less visible to their prey, surrounded as they are by the shadows of a jungle."

"Yes, but the leopard is an intelligent animal. It knows— as an example only—to approach its prey from downwind, so that its victims won't know it's there. Given that obvious degree of intelligence, it surely requires no stretch of the imagination to conclude that, if a leopard happens to be born in a jungle without spots, it will simply move to an environment where it will be less visible: a desert, for example, if its coat is tawny; or to any other place where it will be less visible. Nature itself, it seems to me, places a premium on intelligence. Why do you think that is?"

"Well, I see your point," he conceded. "And yet, intelligence, too, is a matter of mechanics: of a plus b equaling c. Computers can do that better than we can."

"Yes, but they can't *feel*. Nor are they self-aware: a computer can't be made that is self-conscious. Intelligence alone doesn't produce self-consciousness. Nor does complexity. We see that in the case of the earthworm."

"Yes, I concede that point also," he admitted. "But what, then, is at the heart of it all? If all living beings have feeling, and are also self-aware, are you suggesting that feeling and self-awareness are at the core of evolution? This strikes at the very heart of Darwin's theory of evolution, a cornerstone of modern science. His system is considered a fundamental truth of modern science, and not a theory at all."

"What I'm suggesting is that Darwin was only offering us a coherent explanation for the mechanics of evolution—the *how* of it, maybe. But he didn't explain the *why*."

"Does there even need to be a why?"

"That is a question we human beings cannot help asking. We'll never be satisfied without reasons. Instinctively, I think, we all know that life does have a purpose, and that it has also meaning. It is much more satisfying, surely, to explain evolution as a reaching upward for ever-greater consciousness. That is the process we see on all sides of us in the evolution of life. Darwin was antediluvial in his thinking! We know, now, that matter itself is only a vibration of energy. How, then, can life itself be determined only by material considerations?

"But consider another aspect of the problem," I continued: "How did conscious life even get started on this planet?"

He considered the question a moment. "Well, some say the germs of it may have come here from another planet."

"That," I scoffed, "is simply begging the question. How did it get started *anywhere*?"

"I must admit you have a point there."

"Moreover, and although the subject is still controversial, innumerable thousands of reputedly credible people claim to have seen UFOs, as they are called, and many have also seen the beings who come in those UFOs. None of those beings looks startlingly different from ourselves. Most of them in fact, from the reports I have read, look very similar to us. How could that be, since they must have evolved quite on their own?"

"Yes, that simple fact makes me doubt their existence."

"Yes, I suppose you'd have to, since it testifies absolutely against evolution being just an accident!"

"One thing I like about Darwin's Theory of Evolution is that it is elegant! It appeals so perfectly to reason."

"Then can't you see the even greater elegance in the thought of consciousness reaching up toward ever-greater *self-awareness*? And then *outward* into an ever-more-greatly expanded sense of what that self entails?"

"But how can I accept your suggestion that consciousness isn't just produced by the brain?"

"By seeing the earthworm, which doesn't even have what we'd call a brain at all, yet is obviously, to some degree, conscious—and even self-conscious enough to wriggle away when it is touched or pricked with a pin."

"Then what *is* consciousness?"

"Consciousness is self-existent. It takes consciousness even to ask the question. People wrongly imagine that everything can be analyzed. In fact, consciousness can't be analyzed, because it can't be broken up into pieces. It simply *is*. Even people who are brain-dead, their brain graphs showing not a single wave of movement, have been shown by scientific experiment to be aware. Life is not *created*: it can only be manifested. To me, this overview of life and evolution is much more elegant than Darwin's theory, and it explains how life even—anywhere, as well as on this planet—got its start. Consciousness is inherent even in the rocks! Its existence there is even dimmer than in the worm, but rocks, and metals too, have been found to respond to stimuli. Tools used in factories have been found to respond better if, from time to time, they are given a rest; they, too, can experience fatigue! This entire universe is alive! It is a manifestation of Higher Consciousness—of God, if you will! And that Consciousness, self-defined because self-existent, is everywhere."

"Then God, to your way of thinking, isn't really a person. Well, but how, then, can He respond to our little human prayers? I maintain, if He exists, that He doesn't even hear them."

"Yet to be infinitely large implies also to be infinitesimally small—to be centered at every point in space."

"This is all incredible. Yet it holds together: It *is* elegant!"

"What could be more elegant than the thought of consciousness struggling upward through evolving material manifestations, to express itself fully at last *as* consciousness! Human beings, everywhere throughout space, look like human beings for the simple reason that their bodies in the astral world are all the same. There exists a beginning 'model' for them, on a higher level of existence. This explanation holds together perfectly!"

"All right, then, what has this to do with your lady of Guadalupe? I gather that you in some way equate her with God. How can that be?"

"She is a manifestation of the mother-aspect of God. God may indeed be visualized also as the Mother of the universe. That's a human concept, but God, being infinitesimally small as well as cosmically vast, can also come to us in any form we human beings find attractive. *Yes* 'He' hears our prayers! He is omniscient. He, or She, responds to them too, when they are sincere."

"So your pilgrimage to Guadalupe is not a complete pipe dream! It has some logic to it."

"Logic, yes, but more than logic. She has appeared to me more than once, and it wasn't my imagination. She responded to real situations in my life. Logic is transcended by love."

"Well, your sincerity is patent. I'm not so sure I don't prefer your beliefs to mine. Thank you for sharing your insights with me."

"You have helped me, too. For I understand better now where I came from, and why. All life, I have realized for some time, is a quest for self-understanding. And all life is a pilgrimage, even if most people have yet to become aware of the fact. That 'self' that I am trying to understand manifests basically, I think, as a simple impulse: the impulse to grow upward and reach out, like a plant, toward the light of ever-higher awareness."

The Schoolteacher

M Y NEXT MEANINGFUL ENCOUNTER WAS WITH A
schoolteacher. There were two people in the front
seat of the car that stopped: a man and a woman. I got in
behind.

The man, without preamble, said, "We're glad to have a
third person here to help arbitrate a discussion we've been
having."

"Well, I'd be happy to try," I said. "What's the discussion
about?"

"My wife Lisa, here, is a schoolteacher, and she's having
lots of trouble with some of the parents of the children she
teaches. All the parents seem to want their children to be
child prodigies; to get into prestigious universities; to shine.
And their poor children are bowed down by the pressure
placed on them."

"My problem," said his wife, "is that they aren't allowed
simply to be children! The parents want information to be
crowded into their heads. And the children are taught to
thrust themselves forward. Phil, my husband here, insists

that life itself *is* competitive, and that children need to prepare early for the real world they'll enter one day."

"Yes," said Phil. "The problem is, competition is the main
reality in today's world. If a person doesn't accept that life
is a rat race, he is left behind. Others get the orders to fill.
Others get the promotions. Others get the recognition. And
the non-combatants get lost in the shuffle."

"But in this way," his wife said, "children never get to
enjoy childhood."

"I don't know about that," said Phil. "It seems to me that a
competitive spirit is very much part of the process of growing
up. Children seem naturally competitive with one another."

"It's in their nature, I grant you," I remarked. "But the job
of those who teach them is surely to show them how to be
better human beings, and not to encourage them to become
bullies."

"Exactly!" said Lisa. "Too much emphasis on cramming
information into their heads, on preparing them for exams,
on teaching them how to win against others, deprives them
of that other side of childhood: the laughter, the gaiety, the
sheer fun of living, and the delight children take in just
playing."

"I must say," I commented, "I agree with you. Moreover,
children need to learn the beauty of cooperation also. One
can accomplish much more, even in the so-called 'real' world
you talk about, Phil, if one can learn to work *with* people,
instead of against them. Not only is harmony more conducive to happiness, but it is more conducive to real success in
life. Let us say you live in a village of one thousand people,
and have a competitive attitude. You will then have nine

hundred and ninety-nine enemies—or at least, competitors. Wouldn't it be better to have nine hundred and ninety-nine friends? Wouldn't all of you be more productive together, as friends, than you could possibly be wasting your group energy in merely trying to best one another?"

"Well," said Phil, "it's by competition that people are forced to try to achieve excellence."

"And yet," I said, "it's an excellence they achieve on their own. I know that there are books on management that counsel leaders to impress their authority on others by shouting occasionally, slamming the phone down, getting angry. Yet people only try to work *around* such adolescent behavior: they never respect it. The best bosses are those who can get their subordinates to work under them *willingly*, not those who have to be coerced. The best bosses are those who can bring out in others a spirit of cooperation. Children, too, need to be taught how to work *with* others, not against them."

"Well, there are plenty of books on management that counsel people just the opposite."

"Well, ask yourself this question: Which attitudes motivates you the most: fear? or a wish to express yourself creatively?"

"Well, fear can be a powerful motivator!"

"Fear also paralyzes. It prevents creativity, and forces people to follow the path of habit and of ingrained custom. How can an organization really flourish, if it is incapable of making the best of fresh opportunities, staying only in the well-worn grooves of the past?"

"Yes, I see your point. From this point of view, a supportive manager will surely be able to get the best out of his subordinates."

"In fact," I said, "the best kind of manager is one who doesn't see those working under him as subordinates at all: who sees them as co-workers in a joint project. He solicits their advice, and listens to their ideas. He doesn't present himself as the true originator of others' ideas; instead, he gives credit where credit is due. Those who work under such a person will try to shine by their creative proposals, and not by putting others down. They will not try to best others. They will be more likely to try to support one another. By competition, on the other hand, they will block one another's' energy: like two hands pushing on a door from opposite sides instead of pushing together on one side."

"What I feel," said Lisa, "is that when children are only crammed with knowledge, and taught to compete with one another so as to get ahead, it not only encourages them to be bullies, but it doesn't develop their latent creativity."

"I agree with you," I said. "A child who can be taught to *enjoy* the learning process is much more certain to enjoy continuing the process throughout his life. I myself was home schooled. It amazed me to meet children from public schools who said they hated school. To me, learning was an adventure."

"A man after my own heart!" she said. "Phil, you're my husband, but can't you see that everyone will get more out of what he's doing if he enjoys doing it?"

"I do see that," answered Phil. "If schooling can be made enjoyable, surely the children will learn more, and better. But how will you make schooling enjoyable? Basic arithmetic must simply be learned by rote; there's no other way of learning it. How are you going to make the multiplication tables interesting?"

"Well," I said, "you can apply them to living situations: to speak of loaves of bread, for instance; or to show how, if they get their multiplication wrong, they may end up cheating themselves."

"But the main thing wrong with formal education," said Lisa, "is that children are taught facts, but are not taught how to absorb or use those facts. Facts are left to stand by themselves, but children are not taught to evaluate them. They learn that Napoleon conquered most of Europe: they are not shown that his attitude of conquest, which eventually brought about his downfall, was therefore a cautionary tale of how not to behave. They are taught about economic depressions: but again as facts, only. They are not taught why such depressions sometimes occur, and how they might be prevented. The depressions themselves are given as facts, only. Students get no idea of the actual suffering a depression can inflict on people, and how that suffering might be alleviated. They are not taught the fundamental cause of depressions: greed. Worst of all, children are not taught how they themselves might find the greatest happiness in life. They are taught that money and success and power will make them happy—but these things have never been found to do so!"

I concurred heartily. "The most important thing," I said, "is to teach them how to be happy regardless of their outer circumstances. And another thing: Which is more important to them: an abundance of facts? or the ability to summon up those facts when they need them? a plethora of facts? or to teach them the concentration required to *absorb* those facts? Efficiency experts go into factories to ascertain how best to improve the work flow. We need to teach children how to become *efficient* in the use of whatever knowledge they are taught."

"Yes," agreed Lisa. "Otherwise, they may just become overburdened with knowledge, and never learn how to use any of it."

"The most important thing of all," I said, "is that they be taught that happiness is the true goal of life. Education should be a means, above all, of learning how to be truly happy!"

"And why should that be the most important thing?" asked Phil.

"Simply because that is the basic motivation underlying everything people do. They think this or that thing or act will bring them happiness, but usually they find, in the end, that their dream was a snare and a delusion. It would help children to understand that happiness lies within themselves, not outside. But there's a second reason also: When they are happy, they can learn better and more easily."

"Well, I must admit," Phil said, "that, apart from the purely egoistic satisfaction of winning, success doesn't bring happiness. Rich people are often *less* happy than those who have little."

"I'm glad you said, 'those who have less,' instead of 'those who have nothing,' because simple living is better for most people than poverty. In simplicity, one has enough to keep his body in good health, and to satisfy his basic wants." I paused, then added, "The song, 'I got plenty o' nothin',' was

written by someone who was well to do, not by someone
who really had nothing! The thing is not to depend on anything outward to give one happiness."

"It seems to me," Lisa said, "that basic delusions trick
mankind into following wrong trails—as if there were false
scents, leading to false conclusions. The desire for riches
is a delusion, because it promises everything but actually
provides very little. Another delusion is the desire for power.
And so many children these days get addicted to drugs that,
in the end, destroy their lives."

"Yes," said Phil. "How do delusions like that ever get
started?"

"It seems to me," I answered, "that it takes energy to
spread such mental infections. The criminal element make
money on people's addictions. Apart from trying to cure
people of their addictions, once they've realized the suffering they've brought into their lives, I suggest that the
best way to cure this modern disease of drug addiction
is to make it impractical to bother selling it: to eliminate
the profit motive, in other words. I think it would help to
decriminalize the sale of drugs. Those who are drawn to
use drugs could, with a doctor's prescription, get them at an
easily affordable price from government-sponsored shops
that would make it unprofitable to gangsters and the lower
element to push them. That, plus a campaign to publicize
the pernicious effects of drug usage, would surely reduce
the demand for drugs until at last it became as rare to want
drugs as it is, today, for people to want to chew tobacco."

"Another widespread delusion," said Lisa, "is the belief
that sex indulgence gives happiness. Children need sex edu-

cation to prevent them from idealizing sexuality. Instead, literature and advertising lean heavily on sexual attraction to promote whatever they may be selling. Even things completely unrelated to sex, like beer or warm clothing, are touted as being 'sexy.' That adjective is applied to anything the advertisers want to make appealing. Yet, in fact, sexuality can be depleting, and marriages with sex for their basic justification usually end in disillusionment, disharmony, mutual distaste, and unhappiness."

"Are you sure about that?" asked Phil. "Why, then, do people find it so attractive?"

"Delusion, again," I replied. "One is surrounded by it on all sides, all the time. Mental conditioning constantly holds before us dream-images of satisfactions that never materialize because we can only experience them vicariously, through the senses. And our senses only report to us what they perceive objectively—as if by telephone! They can't touch our inner selves. We are not what we see, hear, smell, taste, and touch. The most beautiful music becomes tiring at last, because it isn't who we really are."

"You know," said Phil, suspending his air of customary cynicism, "if growing children could be taught the importance of sexual restraint, that alone could change modern civilization!"

"Yes," enthused Lisa. "They aren't taught, and by the time life teaches them their need for it, they've already developed unwholesome habits. Sex, although necessary . . ."

". . . and fun," added Phil.

"Yes, pleasurable, yet over-indulgence in it weakens people, and keeps them wallowing in unrefined satisfactions."

I said, "You know, it is common in less civilized societies to have a 'rite of passage' for children on reaching puberty. I don't know whether those societies address sex education, but it would be ideal if they did. There could be a formal ceremony, emphasizing the importance of using the creative impulse wisely: not for pleasure so much as for procreation. All their education, from then on, could incorporate this training, and teach children the physical and psychological benefits *to themselves* of self-control. In this way they could be initiated into the mystery of what it truly means to be an adult: how self-control can help one to become the master of his own destiny."

Phil exclaimed, "This is wonderful! What you've suggested to us is a system that would make for a truly harmonious society."

"And one," adjoined Lisa, "in which people thought more of giving outwardly than of taking greedily for themselves!"

"Schools," I said, "should be places where children learn above all how to 'school' themselves: how to control themselves; how to be harmonious in themselves, and harmonious, consequently, with others."

"That's the kind of schooling," Lisa exclaimed, "that I wish I could share with children. Instead, parents themselves demand that we cram their children's heads with unnecessary knowledge, and school them in attitudes that cannot but lead them, in the end, to dissatisfaction and unhappiness. But how can we start such a movement?"

"The only way I can think of," I said, "is to offer individual examples—to start new schools on the order of what we're all proposing here. If these schools can prove that children become *more* successful in the competitive modern world, parents themselves will clamor for such schooling for their children. Examples will tell much more than a thousand theoretical words. If this system can be shown to work, everyone will embrace it. It will take time, but surely, in time and if it does work, it will be accepted everywhere."

"Certainly," added Phil, "the old system is producing many failures. People who come through it unscathed show not so much the efficacy of the system as their own innate ability. Some people succeed *in spite of* the training they receive. But if you look at the average product of modern education, I think it will have to be admitted that the results are not good."

"Yes," I said, "there are altogether a depressing number of childhood suicides, and children grow up as atheists with no high ideals. Given no ideals to work towards, they may sink into an apathy of world rejection that is, in itself, far from an inducement to success. I would say that modern society is on a completely unwholesome descent into rejection, not affirmation. Without a positive outlook, and without positive expectations of life, how can there be success of any kind? Only those with the lowest ideals can get anywhere!"

"I'm glad we picked you up!" declared Phil.

"Yes," said Lisa, "I think I see the way, now, to a new hope for education."

"You have both helped me, too," I said. "For now I see a way more clearly to the creation of a better society. I had been wondering whether there was any hope. Now I see that there is. Thank you!"

EIGHTEEN

The Social Activist

HI!" SAID THE NEXT MAN, AS I GOT INTO THE FRONT
seat beside him. "Name's Frank."

"Friend," I replied. I suspect he hadn't really heard me, for he asked me immediately, "So what is your opinion of the state of the world?"

"That's a broad issue!" I commented with a smile.

"Basically, however, do you think things might be improved?"

"I suppose they might be. But to what things are you referring, specifically?"

"Well, society. The system we're living under. The fact that there's so much poverty everywhere. Everything's wrong: education; government; society; unequal job opportunities—you name it, it's all wrong."

"Well, I suppose we can never really expect perfection in this world."

"Well, if it's imperfect it's up to us to make it perfect!" He said this explosively. "What gets me is people's apathy. Our duty, as human beings, is to make this world a place worth living in."

"Well, certainly we have a duty to improve matters, where we can. But surely we have to reconcile ourselves to the fact that nothing can ever be perfect."

"Why not?" Again, this came out explosively.

"But do you seriously believe that there can be absolutes in this world of relativities?"

"And do you seriously believe there can't be? What about Yes and No? Those are absolutes. They permit no qualifications."

"All right, then, what about, 'Am I alive?' Can you really say, 'Absolutely yes?' Aren't you more alive sometimes than you are at other times? And can you ever answer, 'Absolutely no'? All right, supposing you are physically dead, can you be sure anyone can say of you that your death is absolute? Something has gone away, but where has it gone? If you are your body, then something remains behind, with at least enough life in it to keep the worms busy for awhile! And if you are not this body, how can you say that *you* are dead just because your body has died?"

At this, he broke into a broad smile. "All right!" he said. "I concede your point. Still, there's an absolute need to eradicate poverty."

"But how can that need ever be fulfilled? It depends first on how we define poverty. What does it mean, to be poor? I have known millionaires who felt they needed still more. And I have known poor people who were rich in more important ways than money: ways such as friendship, and peace of mind, and happiness."

"I see what you mean. Then wouldn't you say there's an absolute need to improve things?"

"How can we say so, when we aren't even clear as to what me mean by 'things'? What exactly *are* 'things'? Do you mean material objects? Material conditions? But matter doesn't even exist! It is now known to be only energy in a low state of vibration."

"All right, all right!" Instead of getting flustered, he was clearly enjoying himself. "Let's start over. Tell me, don't you think the social system might be improved?"

"One of the great fallacies of one modern system, communism, is the theory that people can be improved from without. No system can make them any better or any worse than they are already. They are what they are *from inside*. It seems to me what you are trying to do is get rid of darkness by beating at it with a stick. How can you do that? The way to banish darkness is to turn on the light!"

"Then are you saying there's no need to concentrate on wrongs? How can you even know where to shine your light, if you don't thrust it—your flashlight, if you will—into the dark corners? You have to see those corners first, to know that they exist."

"Yes, you have me there. We can't ignore evil. We must know that it exists. But then we must ask ourselves, What can we do about it? The way to eradicate unhappiness is by concentrating on happiness. The way to eradicate pain is to concentrate on those things in life which give you a sense of inner freedom. The way to eradicate darkness, I repeat, is to concentrate on that which gives light."

"So then, the best way to correct the imperfection in our

system of education is to concentrate on finding a better system, and not to protest against the inadequacies in the present system? Well, yes, I must agree with you there. And the best way to improve society in general is not to point out what's wrong with it now? Is that what you're saying?"

"Yes, I guess I've said that . . ." I began, when he pounced with the triumphant cry, "So then, how can you even try to improve anything, if you won't admit there's anything wrong in the first place?"

We shared a good laugh together.

"All right, yes," I conceded, "we must know that wrong is there. And we must know why it's wrong. I guess what I'm saying is that it's all relative. But its relativity is not absolute! It's directional! I can be continuously more and more wrong, or (conversely) less and less wrong, but I can never be absolutely either wrong or not wrong—that is to say, I can never be absolutely right—as long as my rightness is something fixed and immutable. And how can anything be that, in a universe where *everything* is mutable?"

"Wow, you're really boxing me in, aren't you? Are you saying, then, that I may as well leave everything as is? Or are you saying, Try, but don't hope ever to succeed?!"

"I guess I'm saying the latter," I answered. He threw up his hand in a gesture of mock despair. "Then what's the point," he asked, "in even living?"

"That was the very question I asked myself before I set out on the journey I'm taking."

"Yes, what *are* you doing here, walking this road alone. What is your goal?"

"I'm trying to find out why I'm even here, alive in this

non-existent, or at any rate non-material, world. What is the point in trying to improve anything, when no improvement can be stable? What's the point in trying to reach a goal that can't be reached, and that for all I know doesn't even exist? And I think I've found the answer. First of all, the answer won't, and can't, be found anywhere except in my own self. Secondly, what I've been looking for is something that's absolute, also, only in myself. That 'thing' is happiness!"

"Yes, but you've pretty well said that happiness, too, is only relative. Isn't that right?"

"Right," I replied. "But our *need* for happiness is absolute! And that need will never be satisfied if we seek the satisfaction outwardly. Here, in this world, the possibility of satisfaction is relative, and the best that can be said of it is that even that relativity is absolute! Here, relativity is the only 'absolute' there is!"

"Then, why try? I mean, why even try to make this a better world to live in?"

"Because in that very effort we move relatively closer to perfection in ourselves. And even in that thought, all that we can accomplish is to remove the thought of imperfection from our own minds. For perfection can only be attained by realizing that we have it already! The clouds that prevent us from seeing this perfection hover gloomily over the landscape of our own minds, but exist nowhere else.

"I see now," I continued triumphantly, "that there was no pilgrimage to be made, no goal to be reached!" I turned rejoicing to my companion, and to my amazement saw there, not a slightly cynical, furrow-browed man, but a young girl, smiling at me radiantly: The Virgin of Guadalupe!

"And all the people you've met along this journey have been aspects of your own self!" She told me. "I Myself am an aspect of your own Self! I am the Motherhood of God. I embrace the universe. I am the Source of your own being. From Me alone you draw the very power to breathe, to think, to create. Without Me, you could do nothing. Without Me, you wouldn't even exist!"

I write these lines in the ether, in letters of light. Someday, someone will capture them, and will write them down on pages that others can read and benefit from. But those words exist already—in your own Self, even as you read these words.

And suddenly I find myself in the Basilica of Guadalupe. The holy relic is there: I see it, and I flow toward it, my arms outstretched in joyous anticipation. I embrace Thy light. I embrace Thy Bliss. We are. . . .

NINETEEN

A Strange Event

THE FOLLOWING ARTICLE APPEARED ON A BACK page of the leading Spanish-language paper in Mexico City. The date is indeterminate. The following is a translation:

Miraculous Vision— or Mass Hallucination?

Yesterday, in the Basilica of Guadalupe, a large congregation was gathered together, singing a hymn of praise before mass. Suddenly there appeared before them, facing the altar, but gazing upward in apparent rapture, a middle-aged man. His hands were outstretched as if in longing toward the image of Our Lady of Guadalupe.

Equally sudden then was his disappearance. It was as though he had never been there.

The congregation asked themselves afterward, What did this apparition signify? Did it even occur?

The Church has yet to make a pronouncement on this strange event. Until then, it is safer that nothing more be said about it.

About the Author

S WAMI KRIYANANDA IS A DIRECT DISCIPLE OF Paramhansa Yogananda, trained by the great Indian master to spread the life-transforming teachings of Kriya Yoga around the globe. He is widely considered one of the world's foremost experts on meditation, yoga, and spiritual practice, having authored nearly 150 books on these subjects.

Kriyananda is the founder of Ananda Sangha, a worldwide organization committed to the dissemination of Yogananda's teachings. In 1968 he founded Ananda World Brotherhood Village, the first spiritual cooperative community based on Yogananda's vision of "world brotherhood colonies." Today Ananda includes ten spiritual communities in the U.S., Europe, and India, and over 140 meditation groups worldwide.

FURTHER EXPLORATIONS

AUTOBIOGRAPHY OF A YOGI
by Paramhansa Yogananda

Autobiography of a Yogi is one of the best-selling Eastern philosophy titles of all time, with millions of copies sold, named one of the best and most influential books of the twentieth century. This highly prized reprinting of the original 1946 edition is the only one available free from textual changes made after Yogananda's death. Yogananda was the first yoga master of India whose mission was to live and teach in the West.

In this updated edition are bonus materials, including a last chapter that Yogananda wrote in 1951, without posthumous changes. This new edition also includes the eulogy that Yogananda wrote for Gandhi, and a new foreword and afterword by Swami Kriyananda, one of Yogananda's close, direct disciples.

Also available in unabridged audiobook (MP3) format, read by Swami Kriyananda.

PARAMHANSA YOGANANDA
A Biography with Personal Reflections and Reminiscences
Swami Kriyananda

Paramhansa Yogananda's classic *Autobiography of a Yogi* is more about the saints Yogananda met than about himself—in spite of Yogananda's astonishing accomplishments.

Now, one of Yogananda's few remaining direct disciples relates the untold story of this great spiritual master and world teacher: his teenage miracles, his challenges in coming to America, his national lecture campaigns, his struggles to fulfill his world-changing mission amid incomprehension and painful betrayals, and his ultimate triumphant achievement. Kriyananda's subtle grasp of his guru's inner nature reveals Yogananda's many-sided greatness. Includes many never-before-published anecdotes.

Also available in unabridged audiobook (MP3) format.

THE NEW PATH
My Life with Paramhansa Yogananda
Swami Kriyananda

When Swami Kriyananda discovered *Autobiography of a Yogi* in 1948, he was totally new to Eastern teachings. This is a great advantage to the Western reader, since Kriyananda walks us along the yogic path as he discovers it from the moment of his initiation as a disciple of Yogananda. With winning honesty, humor, and deep insight, he shares his journey on the spiritual path through personal stories and experiences.

Through more than four hundred stories of life with Yogananda, we tune in more deeply to this great master and to the teachings he brought to the West. This book is an ideal complement to *Autobiography of a Yogi*.

Also available in unabridged audiobook (MP3) format, read by Swami Kriyananda.

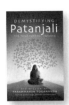

DEMYSTIFYING PATANJALI:
THE YOGA SUTRAS (Aphorisms)
The Wisdom of Paramhansa Yogananda
Presented by his direct disciple, Swami Kriyananda

A great spiritual master of ancient times—Patanjali—enlightened humanity through his *Yoga Sutras* with a step-by-step outline of how all spiritual aspirants achieve union with God. Since then, scholars have written commentaries that bury Patanjali's insights in confusing terms. Now, a modern yoga master—Paramhansa Yogananda—has resurrected Patanjali's original revelations. In *Demystifying Patanjali*, Swami Kriyananda shares Yogananda's crystal clear and easy-to-grasp explanations.

THE ESSENCE OF THE BHAGAVAD GITA
Explained by Paramhansa Yogananda
As Remembered by his disciple, Swami Kriyananda

Rarely in a lifetime does a new spiritual classic appear that has the power to change people's lives and transform future generations. This is such a book.

This revelation of India's best-loved scripture approaches it from a fresh perspective, showing its deep allegorical meaning and its down-to-earth practicality. The themes presented are universal: how to achieve victory in life in union with the divine; how to prepare for life's "final exam," death, and what happens afterward; how to triumph over all pain and suffering.

Also available in unabridged audiobook (MP3) format, read by Swami Kriyananda.

REVELATIONS OF CHRIST
Proclaimed by Paramhansa Yogananda
Presented by his disciple, Swami Kriyananda

The rising tide of alternative beliefs proves that now, more than ever, people are yearning for a clear-minded and uplifting understanding of the life and teachings of Jesus Christ.

This galvanizing book, presenting the teachings of Christ from the experience and perspective of Paramhansa Yogananda, one of the greatest spiritual masters of the twentieth century, finally offers the fresh perspective on Christ's teachings for which the world has been waiting. This book gives us an opportunity to understand and apply the Scriptures in a more reliable way than any other: by studying under those saints who have communed directly, in deep ecstasy, with Christ and God.

Also available in unabridged audiobook (MP3) format, read by Swami Kriyananda.

CONVERSATIONS WITH YOGANANDA
Recorded, Compiled, and Edited with commentary by his disciple, Swami Kriyananda

Here is an unparalleled, first-hand account of the teachings of Paramhansa Yogananda. Featuring nearly 500 never-before-released stories, sayings, and insights, this is an extensive, yet eminently accessible treasure trove of wisdom from one of the 20th century's most famous yoga masters. Compiled and edited with commentary by Swami Kriyananda, one of Yogananda's closest direct disciples.

THE ESSENCE OF SELF-REALIZATION
The Wisdom of Paramhansa Yogananda
Recorded, Compiled, and Edited by his disciple, Swami Kriyananda

With nearly three hundred sayings rich with spiritual wisdom, this book is the fruit of a labor of love. A glance at the table of contents will convince the reader of the vast scope of this work. It offers as complete an explanation of life's true purpose, and of the way to achieve that purpose, as may be found anywhere.

Also available in unabridged audiobook (MP3) format, read by Swami Kriyananda.

WHISPERS FROM ETERNITY
Paramhansa Yogananda
Edited by his disciple, Swami Kriyananda

Many poetic works can inspire, but few, like this one, have the power to change your life. Yogananda was not only a spiritual master, but a master poet, whose verses revealed the hidden divine presence behind even everyday things. This book has the power to rapidly accelerate your spiritual growth, and provides hundreds of delightful ways for you to begin your own conversation with God.

Also available in unabridged audiobook (MP3) format, read by Swami Kriyananda.

~ ~ *The WISDOM of YOGANANDA series* ~ ~

This series features writings of Paramhansa Yogananda not available elsewhere—including many from his earliest years in America—in an approachable, easy-to-read format. The words of the Master are presented with minimal editing, to capture his expansive and compassionate wisdom, his sense of fun, and his practical spiritual guidance.

HOW TO BE HAPPY ALL THE TIME
The Wisdom of Yogananda Series, VOLUME 1, *Paramhansa Yogananda*

Yogananda powerfully explains virtually everything needed to lead a happier, more fulfilling life. Topics include: looking for happiness in the right places; choosing to be happy; tools and techniques for achieving happiness; sharing happiness with others; balancing success and happiness; and many more.

KARMA AND REINCARNATION
The Wisdom of Yogananda Series, VOLUME 2, *Paramhansa Yogananda*

Yogananda reveals the truth behind karma, death, reincarnation, and the afterlife. With clarity and simplicity, he makes the mysterious understandable. Topics include: why we see a world of suffering and inequality; how to handle the challenges in our lives; what happens at death, and after death; and the purpose of reincarnation.

SPIRITUAL RELATIONSHIPS
The Wisdom of Yogananda Series, VOLUME 3, *Paramhansa Yogananda*

This book contains practical guidance and fresh insight on relationships of all types. Topics include: how to cure bad habits that can end true friendship; how to choose the right partner; sex in marriage and how to conceive a spiritual child; problems that arise in marriage; and the Universal Love behind all your relationships.

HOW TO BE A SUCCESS
The Wisdom of Yogananda Series, VOLUME 4, *Paramhansa Yogananda*

This book includes the complete text of *The Attributes of Success*, the original booklet later published as *The Law of Success*. In addition, you will learn how to find your purpose in life, develop habits of success and eradicate habits of failure, develop your will power and magnetism, and thrive in the right job.

HOW HAVE COURAGE, CALMNESS, AND CONFIDENCE
The Wisdom of Yogananda Series, VOLUME 5, *Paramhansa Yogananda*

This book shows you how to transform your life. Dislodge negative thoughts and depression. Uproot fear and thoughts of failure. Cure nervousness and systematically eliminate worry from your life. Overcome anger, sorrow, over-sensitivity, and a host of other troublesome emotional responses; and much more.

HOW TO ACHIEVE GLOWING HEALTH AND VITALITY
The Wisdom of Yogananda Series, VOLUME 6, *Paramhansa Yogananda*

Paramhansa Yogananda, a foremost spiritual teacher of modern times, offers practical, wide-ranging, and fascinating suggestions on how to have more energy and live a radiantly healthy life. The principles in this book promote physical health and all-round well-being, mental clarity, and ease and inspiration in your spiritual life.

Readers will discover the priceless Energization Exercises for rejuvenating the body and mind, the fine art of conscious relaxation, and helpful diet tips for health and beauty.

THE ART AND SCIENCE OF RAJA YOGA
Swami Kriyananda

Contains fourteen lessons in which the original yoga science emerges in all its glory—a proven system for realizing one's spiritual destiny. This is the most comprehensive course available on yoga and meditation today. Over 450 pages of text and photos give you a complete and detailed presentation of yoga postures, yoga philosophy, affirmations, meditation instruction, and breathing practices.

Also included are suggestions for daily yoga routines, information on proper diet, recipes, and alternative healing techniques.

MEDITATION FOR STARTERS *with CD*
Swami Kriyananda

Have you wanted to learn to meditate, but just never got around to it? Or tried "sitting in the silence" only to find yourself too restless to stay more than a few moments? If so, *Meditation for Starters* is just what you've been looking for—and with a companion CD, it provides everything you need to begin a meditation practice.

Filled with easy-to-follow instructions, beautiful guided visualizations, and answers to important questions on meditation, the book includes: what meditation is (and isn't); how to relax your body and prepare yourself for going within; and techniques for interiorizing and focusing the mind.

AWAKEN TO SUPERCONSCIOUSNESS
Swami Kriyananda

This popular guide includes everything you need to know about the philosophy and practice of meditation, and how to apply the meditative mind to resolve common daily conflicts in uncommon, superconscious ways.

Superconsciousness is the hidden mechanism at work behind intuition, spiritual and physical healing, successful problem solving, and finding deep and lasting joy.

LIVING WISELY, LIVING WELL
Swami Kriyananda
Winner of the 2011 International Book Award for
Best Self-Help: Motivational Title

Want to transform your life? Tap into your highest potential?
Get inspired, uplifted, and motivated?

Living Wisely, Living Well contains 366 practical ways to improve your life—a thought for each day of the year. Each reading is warm with wisdom, alive with positive expectation, and provides simple actions that bring profound results. See life with new eyes. Discover hundreds of techniques for self-improvement.

THE RUBAIYAT OF OMAR KHAYYAM EXPLAINED
Paramhansa Yogananda, edited by Swami Kriyananda

The *Rubaiyat* is loved by Westerners as a hymn of praise to sensual delights. In the East its quatrains are considered a deep allegory of the soul's romance with God, based solely on the author Omar Khayyam's reputation as a sage and mystic. But for centuries the meaning of this famous poem has remained a mystery. Now Paramhansa Yogananda reveals the secret meaning and the "golden spiritual treasures" hidden behind the *Rubaiyat's* verses—and presents a new scripture to the world.

THE BHAGAVAD GITA
According to Paramhansa Yogananda
Edited by Swami Kriyananda

Based on the teachings of Paramhansa Yogananda, this translation of the Gita brings alive the deep spiritual insights and poetic beauty of the famous battlefield dialogue between Krishna and Arjuna. Based on the little-known truth that each character in the Gita represents an aspect of our own being, it expresses with revelatory clarity how to win the struggle within us between the forces of our lower and higher natures.

CRYSTAL CLARITY PUBLISHERS

Crystal Clarity Publishers offers additional resources to assist you in your spiritual journey, including many other books, a wide variety of inspirational and relaxation music composed by Swami Kriyananda, and yoga and meditation videos. To see a complete listing of our products, contact us for a print catalog or see our website: www.crystalclarity.com

Crystal Clarity Publishers
14618 Tyler Foote Rd., Nevada City, CA 95959
TOLL FREE: 800.424.1055 or 530.478.7600 / FAX: 530.478.7610

EMAIL: clarity@crystalclarity.com

ANANDA WORLDWIDE

Ananda Sangha, a worldwide organization founded by Swami Kriyananda, offers spiritual support and resources based on the teachings of Paramhansa Yogananda. There are Ananda spiritual communities in Nevada City, Sacramento, Palo Alto, and Los Angeles California; Seattle, Washington; Portland and Laurelwood, Oregon; as well as a retreat center and European community in Assisi, Italy, and communities near New Delhi and Pune, India. Ananda supports more than 140 meditation groups worldwide.

For more information about Ananda Sangha communities or meditation groups near you, please call 530.478.7560 or visit www.ananda.org.

THE EXPANDING LIGHT

Ananda's guest retreat, The Expanding Light, offers a varied, year-round schedule of classes and workshops on yoga, meditation, and spiritual practice. You may also come for a relaxed personal renewal, participating in ongoing activities as much or as little as you wish. The beautiful serene mountain setting, supportive staff, and delicious vegetarian food provide an ideal environment for a truly meaningful, spiritual vacation.

For more information, please call 800.346.5350
or visit www.expandinglight.org